THE ICE CAPTAIN'S DAUGHTER

SUZANNE G. ROGERS

IDUNN COURT PUBLISHING

CONTENTS

Idunn Court Publishing
7 Ramshorn Court
Savannah, GA 31411

ISBN: 978-0-9907561-0-1

Published by Idunn Court Publishing, January 2013

Published in the United States of America
Cover Design: Suzanne G. Rogers
Editor: Kathryn Riley Miller

❀ Created with Vellum

To Juli D. Revezzo,
who always offers a kind word

AN UNEXPECTED ENCOUNTER

*J*illian Roring gazed at the passing Cotswolds scenery through the carriage window. Although the rain-drenched English countryside was lovely, the dreary weather had slackened the horses' pace. Hidden by voluminous skirts and petticoats, Jillian's toes tapped the carriage floor. Her maid looked up from her knitting.

"Are ye troubled about something, Miss Roring?"

"I've never been quite so impatient to get somewhere in my whole life. At this pace, we'll most certainly miss the three o'clock train to London. Have you ever been to town, Betsy?"

"Me and my brother George was born there, in the East End."

"Perhaps you have some friends you'd like to visit, on your days off?"

"No, miss. I promised meself if I ever left, I would ne'er look back. I mean ter keep that promise, no matter what."

"That's quite admirable."

Jillian glanced over at the rapidly increasing length of lace coiled on Betsy's lap.

"You're so very clever with your hands. I've thought about

1

SUZANNE G. ROGERS

learning to knit but I'm afraid your work would put my efforts to shame."

"Ye've employed yer time at the piano much better, ter be sure."

Just then, the brougham slowed abruptly and then came to a stop. The two young women braced their feet on the floor to avoid being thrown forward.

"Oh, bother," Jillian said. "Why are we stopping? We're in the middle of nowhere."

The knitting needles ceased their perpetual motion. Betsy's eyes widened. "Perhaps it's a highwayman!"

Jillian patted her arm. "It's nearly the twentieth century, so I don't suppose highwaymen exist anymore. No, I imagine a broken tree branch has fallen across the road. We'll be on our way momentarily, as soon as George removes it."

When a pistol shot rang out, both women flinched. Moments later, the carriage door was flung open, and a strange man appeared. A kerchief covered the lower half of his face and he brandished a British Bull Dog revolver. Betsy shrieked.

Although Jillian was shaking, she lifted her chin. "What do you mean by this intrusion, sir?"

To Jillian's shock, the man lurched into the carriage and grabbed her by the wrist. "Yer comin' with me, miss."

"I most surely am *not!* Unhand me, blackguard!"

Although she tried to twist away, the highwayman hauled her from the carriage and into the road. From the driver's seat, George was hunched over, clutching his shoulder.

"Don't touch my mistress!" he managed.

The robber gestured toward the young man with his pistol. "Stay where ye are, unless ye want the next bullet in yer heart."

Betsy started to climb out of the brougham, but the robber shook his head. "Yer to deliver the ransom note."

He tossed a crudely written missive at the maid, even as a look of confusion twisted her features.

2

"But I thought I was ter go with—"

"Shut up," he said, pointing his gun at Betsy.

"Don't you dare hurt her!" Jillian exclaimed.

The man chuckled. "Ye should be worried about yerself." He fired another bullet into the air over George's head. "Drive on!"

Startled at the loud noise, the horses backed up. The wooden rear wheel of the carriage rolled over the robber's foot. In the next moment, the horses changed direction and bolted. The man dropped his grip on Jillian's arm as he hopped on one leg, reeling off a litany of curses. Without hesitating, Jillian picked up her full skirts and ran into the woods on the far side of the road.

A desperate glance around revealed no place to hide. Although her bottle green traveling suit blended with the foliage, the trees were too slender to offer refuge.

"Stop or it'll be the worse fer ye!"

A bullet whistled overhead and sent a spray of bark into Jillian's path, but she was undeterred. *I'm not a sea captain's daughter for nothing!* Her boots squelched in the muddy leaves as she ran. Determined to evade her captor, she darted around trees and bushes. Branches plucked at her sleeves and hat, and raindrops blurred her vision. Moisture soaked into her clothes, making her progress ever more labored. Worse, her corset wouldn't allow her to take a deep breath. A sharp cramp in her side finally forced Jillian to pause.

A crashing in the woods nearby startled her into tripping on a felled branch. Moments later, her pursuer yanked her upright and slapped her across the face.

"That's fer the trouble ye caused."

His kerchief slipped with his efforts. Although her eyes stung with tears, Jillian peered at him. *I know him!*

"Sam Netherby, is that you?"

The man swore and jerked his kerchief up over his nose. Jillian pulled the twelve-inch steel hatpin from her beribboned cap and stabbed him in the shoulder with it. Sam howled with pain—and rage—as the hatpin protruded from his body.

"Witch!"

While he was preoccupied with his injury, Jillian took off running once more. A sudden gust of wind lifted her cap from her blonde hair and blew it into a tree. Not twenty paces later, another gunshot rang out. Something tugged at her skirt but she didn't pause. *British Bull Dogs have five rounds...and he's spent four. Let's hope the last one doesn't find its way into my back.*

She emerged from the woods and into a clearing. The rain had become a spring squall, complete with thunder and lightning. Jillian spotted a cottage beyond a rock fence, with a curl of smoke rising from the chimney.

"Help! Somebody help me!"

She sprinted for the stile—too late. Sam grabbed the gathered fabric on the back of her skirt and held her fast.

"Let me *go!*" she screamed.

He grabbed her around the waist and lifted her bodily back toward the line of trees. As she struggled to free herself, a deep, commanding voice rose above the storm.

"Step away from the lady at once!"

Sam's sudden release pitched Jillian forward into the mud, next to a pair of Wellington boots. Blinking away raindrops, she glanced up at a tall, bearded man. He wore a fierce expression and was aiming a hunting rifle at her assailant.

"Place your firearm on the ground," he ordered.

The pistol landed with a splash in a puddle. In the next moment, Jillian's erstwhile kidnapper was hightailing it to the woods. *I'm safe!* A wave of gratitude loosened the knot in Jillian's chest.

"I'm in your debt, sir."

The man lowered his shotgun. "Are you all right, miss?"

"I believe so."

The immediate danger past, Jillian cast an appraising glance at her rescuer. He was hatless and in his shirtsleeves, having come to her aid at a moment's notice. She took his proffered hand, uncomfortably aware her hat was missing, her dress was muddy, and the hair Betsy had so carefully curled and arranged for her that morning now resembled blonde snakes. Jillian attempted a curtsy, but suddenly found herself sitting in mud once more. A streak of lightning lit the sky, followed in the next moment by a tremendous crack of thunder. Her nerves frayed, she burst into tears.

The bearded man set his rifle down, spanned her waist with his large hands, and lifted her to her feet. He jerked his head toward the cottage, shouting to be heard over the storm.

"Come inside."

He retrieved his rifle and Sam's pistol and stepped toward the stile. As Jillian moved to follow, she faltered. A sharp stinging in her leg finally reached her awareness shortly before she fainted.

A PAINFUL ACHE brought Jillian to consciousness. Confused, she raised herself up on an elbow. She was resting on a small bed in the corner of a one-room stone cottage. Her jacket and gloves were draped at the foot of the bed, her right leg was throbbing, and a large reddish-brown streak stained her dress in the vicinity of her thigh. To her alarm, the fabric had been pierced by a small hole. *A bullet hole!*

The man who'd rescued her sat next to the fire, where a skinned rabbit was roasting on a spit over the open flames. He was still hatless, but he'd since donned a lounge jacket. He glanced over when she pushed herself into a sitting position.

"So you're finally awake."

"Was I shot?"

"The bullet only grazed you, but you lost a fair amount of blood. I applied a bandage to stanch the bleeding."

Since the injury was several inches north of her knee, Jillian flushed with embarrassment.

"Thank you," she managed.

He stood and bowed from the waist. "Mr. Mackenzie Logan, at your service."

"Miss Jillian Roring." She nodded. "I'm very pleased to make your acquaintance, sir, and I thank you for your timely intervention. That horrible man was trying to kidnap me."

"I gathered as much."

"I was on my way to the Cirencester train station when my carriage was waylaid. The highwayman is Sam Netherby and he used to work for my uncle before he was fired for drunkenness. Sam was after a ransom, apparently, but I impaled him with my hatpin for his trouble."

"Quick thinking, that. Do you imagine he was working alone?"

"I-I don't know. I didn't see anyone else." She cast a worried glance at the door. "Do you suppose he'll return?"

"Since I have his pistol, I suspect he's long gone. When we reach my home tomorrow, I'll send for the constable."

"This isn't your home?"

"No, it's a hunting cottage on the edge of my estate."

Jillian's throat suddenly contracted with thirst. "May I trouble you for a drink of water?"

"Of course." Logan hastened to pour Jillian a cup of water from a jug. "The rabbit will be cooked in a few minutes, if you're hungry."

After he gave her the water, he sank back into his chair and turned toward the fire. As she drank, Jillian had the opportunity to examine the man's profile. Although he was dressed as a gentleman, his curly chestnut-colored hair was tousled and wild. A full beard obscured the lower half of his face, but his nose might be described as elegant. He'd smiled when he handed her the cup, but no sense of merriment lit his arresting green eyes. In fact, he had the glum demeanor of a man in deep mourning. Logan had shown her every courtesy, but Jillian suddenly had the uncomfortable feeling she was intruding on some unspoken grief. In addition, she shuddered to think what Aunt Letty would say about the impropriety of the situation.

While Logan removed the roasted meat from the spit, Jillian set her cup down on a nearby chair and retrieved the jacket and gloves draped over the foot of the bed. Although she lamented the damp and muddy condition of her jacket, her kidskin gloves were ruined and could not be worn. A powerful thunderclap shook the cottage just then, and she jumped. "Oh, my!"

Logan glanced over. When he noticed the jacket and gloves clutched in Jillian's hands, his eyebrows knit together.

"What are you doing, Miss Roring?"

"I've trespassed too long on your privacy. I really must let my family know where I am."

"I'm afraid this storm prevents us from traveling tonight."

"Oh, I didn't mean that you should trouble yourself. There are still a few hours of light left. I believe I can find my way back to the road."

"Don't be ridiculous. Even if you managed to avoid being struck by lightning, you shouldn't put weight on your extremity."

Although she didn't want to admit it, Jillian knew Logan was right. The slightest movement of her leg was agony. To her horror, tears welled up in her eyes and spilled down her cheeks.

"S-Sorry," she managed. Despite her best efforts, her self-control kept slipping from her grasp, and a sob escaped her lips. "Forgive me."

"There's no need."

Logan retrieved her cup and took it to a rough-hewn side-board. There, he poured out a sizable amount of amber liquid from a glass bottle sitting on top. He brought it back to Jillian and held the cup to her lips as if she were a young child.

"Drink this. You've had quite a shock."

She took the cup from him and gulped the contents. When she gasped and coughed afterwards, Logan laughed and patted her on the back.

"You shouldn't have downed it all in one go."

"I thought it was medicine!" she gasped.

A shudder shook her frame and Logan took the cup before she dropped it.

"Many people consider brandy medicinal, Miss Roring, but it's meant to be savored." Still smiling, he set the cup aside. "Have you never had spirits before?"

"A half glass of wine with dinner upon occasion."

Jillian rested her face in her hands, suddenly woozy. Logan helped her lie back and drew the covers up over her shoulders.

"I'll hang your jacket by the fire so it will be dry by morning. Hopefully the storm will have passed by then and I can take you to a telephone."

For some reason, Jillian found forming words increasingly difficult. "Marvelous invention…telephone," she murmured.

"Sleep now. Upon my word as a gentleman, you have nothing to fear."

Although she had only just met Logan, Jillian felt safe. *This will sort itself out in the morning, and I'll resume my journey to London with an adventure to tell.* Her eyes closed. *At least I made the man laugh*, she thought as she drifted off into a deep slumber.

LOGAN ATE his dinner at the small table underneath the window. The squall rattled the glass panes, but he paid little attention. Instead, he found his gaze drawn to the young sleeping beauty fate had thrown in his path. Her clear complexion had been rendered pale by her ordeal, and her white-blonde hair lay across the pillow like corn silk. Admittedly, when he'd dressed her wound it had been difficult to keep his attention from wandering. He was far too gentlemanly, however, to dwell on inappropriate thoughts about helpless young women. His beard twitched as he pictured her wielding her hatpin as a weapon. *Perhaps the lady is not so helpless after all?*

As bedraggled as she was at present, Miss Roring appeared to be well bred and genteel. Although her hat was missing, her dress, petticoat, and shoes were fashioned of the finest materials. She was most likely an heiress or under the protection of someone with money. Logan shook his head with dismay at her predicament. *Gah! England has run amuck with thieves, pickpockets, and opportunists.*

Another explosive torrent of rain reminded Logan his horse needed attention. He stepped into the boots sitting next to the door, shrugged on his overcoat, and headed outside toward the small stable adjacent to the cottage. When he returned twenty minutes later, damp and chilled, the girl was still asleep. Logan threw a few logs on the fire and settled down in his chair with a blanket. He gazed at his guest as he waited for sleep to claim him. *She's extraordinarily pretty and unspoiled. It's too bad she's traveling to town. London society will leave her jaded and heartbroken... like me.* His eyelids slid shut.

IDUNN COURT

*A*lthough the room at the roadside inn was dark and shabby, it was greatly brightened by the strewn contents of a hand-tooled leather trunk. Finery lay about, as if the trunk had exploded in an excess of merriment. Clad in an exquisitely tailored tea gown and feathered hat, Betsy danced around in her bare feet. She paused every so often to drink from the uncorked bottle in her hand. Just when she'd added a lace-trimmed fan to her ensemble, a key rasped in the lock and the door opened. George appeared. As he caught a glimpse of Betsy, a broad grin lit his face.

"Oi, don't ye look grand!"

Betsy dropped into an exaggerated curtsy.

"Thank ye kindly, brother. Would ye care for a bit o' refreshment?"

She tapped the bottle with the fan, in invitation.

"Don't mind if I do. Ye look like you've had a wee head start." George took a long pull and smacked his lips with satisfaction. "I done posted the ransom note off ter Sir William."

"He'll be a mite put out when he reads it." Betsy's giggle ended in a snort.

"And I got a pretty penny for the brougham, too, though not as much as it's worth. We won't be needin' it where we're goin'."

Betsy hiccupped. "I'm not leavin' England without Sam."

"Don't fret. We're not settin' sail until we've had our share o' the ransom."

"Ye were brilliant, by the way." She giggled. "For a moment I thought ye really *had* been shot. When we get ter America, maybe ye should become an actor."

"Aye, I might fancy that."

"And if Sam won't marry me, I'll find somebody with money who will."

He snickered. "Ye'd best marry someone daft, then. Nobody else will mistake ye for a lady, despite your fine purloined feathers."

Betsy snatched the hat from her head and began whacking George with it. She chased him around the room until a banging came on the door. They stopped dead and exchanged a horrified look.

"Coppers?" Betsy whispered.

"Can't be!"

The banging continued, accompanied by the sound of a familiar voice.

"Open up."

Wide-eyed, George threw the door open. An exasperated Sam strode into the room. "Did ye post the ransom note ter Sir William yet?"

"Yeah, an hour ago," George said.

Sam cursed, grabbed the bottle of liquor from George, and drained it.

"What're ye doin' here?" Betsy asked, aghast. "We didn't expect to see ye till Liverpool."

"We said we'd meet up here if somethin' went wrong. The girl got away."

"Ye dolt!" George exclaimed.

Sam shoved him. "If ye hadn't backed the carriage over my foot, she wouldn't have done!"

George returned the shove. "Nobody asked ye ter stand so close, ye fool!"

"Stop!" Betsy pried the two men apart. "Tell us what happened, Sam."

"The she-devil ran off and when I grabbed her, she stabbed me with this." Sam opened his jacket, where he'd woven the hatpin into the inside lining of his jacket. A spot of dried blood was visible on his shirt.

Betsy gasped. "Are ye all right?"

"Aye, but she saw my face. Then we run smack into a gent with a Purdy shotgun. I near got my backside ventilated."

Sam began to pace back and forth in the ensuing silence. Betsy pushed her fingertips against her temples as if to quell the onset of a headache. George folded his arms across his chest, drilled Sam with a level stare, and waited.

"Nobody knows ye two are involved," Sam said finally. "Ye can drive the brougham back to Gloucester and put this business all on me."

"That's brilliant," George snapped. "We can't go back. I already done sold the brougham, like we planned."

"I should have done her in right off and dragged the body into the woods. The rain woulda washed away the blood in no time."

"What a minute…what's this about doin' Miss Roring in? I thought ye were holdin' her fer ransom," Betsy said, taken aback.

"Don't be daft. I never had any intention ter hand her over alive. As it is, she's a loose end."

Sam passed a shaking hand over his face. Betsy squeezed his arm.

"Don't despair. That hatpin will fetch a few quid. Them is real diamonds. And I also have Miss Roring's gold earbobs. Between the three of us, we might have money enough fer passage ter America."

"You reckon so?" As Sam peered at her, the pinched look on his face eased.

"We can always roll a few swells in Liverpool," George said.

A smile lifted the corners of Sam's mouth. "That we can, laddie."

"I'm a fair pickpocket, I am," Betsy said.

Sam chuckled. "All right. We'll ride fer Swindon at dawn and take the train ter Liverpool. After that, we'll buy tickets on the first ship sailin' west."

Betsy threw her arms around Sam's neck and planted a kiss on his mouth. "We're ter be married when we get ter America, promise?"

Sam disentangled himself.

"Aye, sure. Right now I'm headed ter the tavern for a pint or three."

After Sam left, George blew out a long breath. Betsy peered at him.

"Ye got that look on yer face, Georgie. What're ye thinkin'?"

"Seems ter me, little sister, that yer boyfriend has become a liability. If Miss Roring saw his face, the coppers'll be after him."

"What're ye goin' on about?"

"Maybe he should meet with a little accident."

Betsy clutched her brother's arm. "No, Georgie. I love him."

He leveled a cool stare at his sister. "Aye? That makes one of us."

WHEN LOGAN WOKE, the cottage windows were glistening with the light of a clear morning. Miss Roring was leaning over the washbasin, splashing her face with water. He stretched to unwind the kinks in his neck and back.

"Good morning. How are you feeling, Miss Roring?" he asked.

Startled by the sound of his voice, she hastened to dab at her damp face with a cloth.

"Good morning, Mr. Logan. I confess my wound hurts abominably."

"I should check your bandage."

A flush suffused her face, and she shrank back. "I, er, I'm certain that isn't necessary."

"I'll be the judge of that."

"No, really, it's fine."

He lifted an eyebrow. "The wound is in danger of infection. If said infection should take hold, you may lose your extremity and ultimately your life. Now sit down and let me have a look at it."

As she hobbled to the bed, he moved over to the washbasin to cleanse his hands. When he turned back to Miss Roring, she'd arranged her skirts to reveal as little of her anatomy as possible. While he unwrapped the bandage, he tried to take her mind off her obvious embarrassment.

"When I was five, my parents gave a dinner party at Idunn Court. All sorts of important people were invited, including a few dukes, duchesses, and lords. The governess was busy, so I dressed myself in an old sailor suit and went outside to climb trees. When I was called inside to meet our illustrious company, I stood in the center of the room and bowed to everyone, not realizing my sailor suit had split up the seam in back and I'd failed to wear an undergarment."

Despite herself, Jillian burst into peals of laughter.

"You might find it amusing, but the vicar's wife did not. She fainted into the pudding and caused a dreadful uproar. The vicar thought I'd done it all on purpose, of course, and so never forgave me. Neither did the governess." Logan rewrapped the bandage, sat back and smiled. "We are done."

Jillian promptly smoothed her petticoat and skirt into place. "Well?"

"The healing process is progressing nicely, but you should stay off your feet to prevent bleeding. The ride to my home is relatively short. We'll be there before breakfast and I will summon a surgeon to attend you."

"You're very considerate." She paused. "Was that story true?"

"Every word. I'm going outside to ready your transportation, Miss Roring. Please don't move around while I'm gone."

ALTHOUGH SHE WAS impatient to leave, Jillian forced herself to sit still. A sense of gratitude washed over her. Logan might be a bit wild in his appearance and somewhat melancholy, but he'd shown her a great deal of kindness...particularly with his bedside manner. *Oh, this is such a big mess...and it's my fault. If I hadn't had my heart set on going to London, nobody would have been shot or inconvenienced.* She took a moment to say a prayer for poor George and Betsy's well-being. She knew Sam only in passing, but found it difficult to believe he'd acted in such a nefarious fashion. *I hope he repents of his wickedness.*

Logan ducked his head as he stepped through the doorway, lest he strike the doorframe with his forehead.

"If you are ready, Miss Roring?"

She stood in a wobbly fashion, but in the next moment she was lifted into the air by the Logan's steely strong arms.

"My heavens!" she gasped. "I believe I can walk a little."

"Doctor's orders."

Logan ducked sideways through the door and set her gently down into the back of a cart lined with clean straw. She gaped at the glossy black stallion strapped into the leather harness in front. His long tail swished to and fro, and he pawed the ground with his forelimbs.

"What a magnificent creature!"

"That's Tuxano. Excuse me a moment."

Logan disappeared into the cottage, reemerging moments later with his top hat in place. He locked the door, mounted Tuxano with athletic grace, and urged the horse into a fast walk. The initial discomfort Jillian experienced as she rode in the rickety cart fled as the gorgeous scenery mesmerized her. The sky was a cloudless masterpiece of blue, and a pleasant breeze meant spring was well underway. The surrounding trees were putting forth shoots, and wildflowers were beginning to wake from their winter slumber.

Beyond the trees, an expanse of pasture rolled gently as far as she could see. In the distance, a herd of deer grazed in the field. The graceful animals suddenly stood stock-still and stared in her direction, as if they could feel her eyes upon them. Tuxano trotted along without pause, however, and the deer resumed their meal. The next pasture was dotted with sheep, their fat, white coats begging to be shorn. Despite her worries and the continuing ache in her leg, Jillian smiled with pleasure.

Tuxano kept a good pace, and they arrived at Logan's home within the half hour. Jillian gasped with delight at her first glimpse of Idunn Court, which radiated charm and warmth. The house itself was three stories, and much of the warm yellow stonework was covered with ivy. The main dwelling was situated on a large courtyard, next to a gurgling stream. Several outlying buildings formed a square. Logan rode Tuxano into the courtyard through the gatehouse.

As the horse and cart came to a halt, servants surged from the structure. Logan reeled off orders to an older woman Jillian assumed was the housekeeper.

"Good morning, Mrs. Lyman. Call Mr. Jones immediately, and then prepare a guest room for Miss Roring."

"Right away, Mr. Logan."

As the woman bustled off, Logan lifted Jillian from the cart.

"Before you take me to my room, may I first use your telephone?" she asked. "My family will be frantic."

"Of course."

From the privacy of Logan's study, Jillian first called Aunt Letty. Since the connection was scratchy and her aunt was excited, she had to repeat her story several times.

"Mr. *Mackenzie* Logan, did you say?" Aunt Letty asked.

"Yes. I'm at his home outside Cirencester. Are you acquainted with him?"

"Only by reputation, child. This is horrible news, I'm afraid, on top of everything else."

"What do you mean?"

"That's not important right now. I'll catch the train to Cirencester this afternoon. My brother will meet me there with a carriage."

"Uncle William must be terribly worried."

"He's been calling every two hours, hoping for good news. I'm going to ring him now and tell him you're safe."

Her aunt severed the connection and Jillian was left to wonder if she'd misunderstood her. What horrible news could Aunt Letty be referring to?

Logan was standing by when she emerged from the study.

"Did you manage to reach your family?" he asked.

"My aunt, Mrs. Marsh, is taking the afternoon train from London to fetch me, and my uncle, Sir William Monroe, will pick her up at the station."

"I look forward to meeting them. Now, let me see you to your room so you can rest."

He carried Jillian up the stairs to the second level, where the housekeeper was airing out a room. Logan deposited Jillian gently on the four-poster bed.

"Find something fresh for our guest to wear, Mrs. Lyman,

while you clean her gown. And bring breakfast on a tray," he said, oblivious to the housekeeper's scowl of disapproval.

"As you wish, sir."

"If you will excuse me, Miss Roring," he said. "Mrs. Lyman here will see to your needs."

"Thank you so much, Mr. Logan. I'm quite grateful for your assistance," Jillian said.

He made her a bow and swept past Mrs. Lyman on his way from the room. Jillian assumed the woman's sour expression had something to do with the mud flaking off her skirt and boots.

"I'm awfully sorry about the dirt," Jillian said. "I had a bit of a scrape on the road yesterday in the storm, and Mr. Logan came to my rescue."

"It's certainly none of my nevermind, miss. I'll send Mary to clean up after you."

With a contemptuous glare, the housekeeper turned on her heel and left without another word. Astonished at the woman's rudeness, Jillian could only stare at her retreating back. Granted, her appearance was in disarray, but it was hardly intentional. Jillian tried to shrug off the slight. Perhaps Mrs. Lyman was disagreeable to everyone.

Despite the pain in her leg, she hobbled to the window. The stream flowing past the house was flanked by lush, grassy banks and spreading trees. A charming stone bridge was situated off to one side. The serene view brought a smile to her face. How could anyone be melancholy or dour for long in a place such as this?

A few minutes later, a young servant came to the door with a dressing gown over her arm. The girl, who spoke with an Irish accent, helped Jillian remove her soiled clothes.

"My name is Mary. I'll be taking yer things downstairs to be sponged and pressed now, but I'll be back with yer breakfast in a jiffy. You're welcome ter use the late Mrs. Logan's dressing gown until yer clothes are clean."

After a brief curtsy, Mary left with the mud-streaked traveling suit. Jillian climbed onto the bed and tried to rest, but her wound made it difficult to relax. At least she finally knew the reason for Logan's air of mourning.

He must have loved his wife very much.

THAT WOMAN

*T*he surgeon, Mr. Jones, arrived at Idunn Court midmorning, and was shown to Jillian's room. Since the surgeon was an elderly man, Jillian was not as mortified to have him tend her wound as she had been with Logan.

"I've never treated a bullet wound on a female before," he said, swabbing the injury with carbolic acid. "Fortunately, it's little more than a deep scratch. Keep it clean and dry, and you'll be right as rain very soon."

"May I walk or will it start bleeding again?"

"If you lie still today, I see no reason you can't move around a bit tomorrow. No footraces, though."

The frighteningly red gouge in her skin made her shudder. "Will I have a scar?"

"Most likely." He chuckled at her crestfallen expression. "Don't be overly concerned, Miss Roring. 'Tis nothing that won't be concealed until the wedding night, eh?"

She felt her cheekbones burn. "I suppose so."

He gave her a drop of laudanum for the pain, wrapped her leg with a fresh bandage and left extra gauze and carbolic acid at her bedside so she could tend the wound herself. Slightly

21

dizzy from the effects of the laudanum, Jillian lay back. She drifted off to sleep finally, and dreamed of a tea party with lambs, fawns, and talking bears.

~

WHEN LOGAN EMERGED from his bath, the full-length mirror revealed how unkempt his appearance had become. His curly hair was far too long and his beard was bushy. No wonder Miss Roring had attempted to flee his company the day before. She would rather have braved the lightning storm than spend one more minute in the company of a brooding hermit.

As his manservant gave him a shave and a haircut, Logan's thoughts wandered to his guest. The young woman had piqued his curiosity, and he wanted to learn more about her background. Her forthright manner, bravery, and resourcefulness were rarities among the women he'd known—and a refreshing change.

The sensation of clean fine linen felt good against his skin. He'd lost quite a bit of weight during his self-imposed exile, so his manservant had to adjust the waistband of his striped trousers. Logan left his bedchamber just as the surgeon emerged from Jillian's room.

"Thank you for coming, Mr. Jones. How is Miss Roring?"

"Let me assure you, Mr. Logan, she will suffer no lasting ill effects from her injury."

"I'm very glad to hear it. The highwayman who attacked her also shot the carriage driver. The driver's gone missing, I'm afraid. Did you happen to treat him?"

"Can't say I did. The last gunshot wound I saw in Cirencester was two years ago, when Lord Lansing's gamekeeper accidentally discharged a hunting rifle at a large boulder. The ricocheting buckshot pierced his right buttock." The surgeon shook his head and chuckled. "His wife never let him forget that."

Logan was puzzled. The road past his estate led directly through Cirencester. Wouldn't Miss Roring's driver have sought medical assistance there—if indeed he'd been shot?

Logan escorted Mr. Jones to his gig parked in the courtyard, and then headed inside to ring the constable. Mrs. Lyman waylaid him en route to his study.

"If I may have a word with you, sir?"

"Why, of course."

Although the housekeeper had never been an effervescent soul, Logan noticed her tone was more clipped than usual. He followed her into his study and shut the door. Never one to mince words, Mrs. Lyman unbridled her tongue immediately.

"I cannot countenance your bringing a trollop into this house."

Logan's mouth fell open in shock, but Mrs. Lyman scarcely drew breath.

"Your mother and father would roll over in their graves if they knew Idunn Court had been so besmirched."

"A trollop? Surely you cannot be referring to Miss Roring!"

The housekeeper's nostrils flared. "Indeed I am."

Logan had difficulty keeping his countenance.

"Mrs. Lyman, let me set your mind at ease. Miss Roring is a gentlewoman of good breeding and the highest morals. She was traveling to the train station yesterday afternoon when a highwayman accosted her very near my hunting cottage. A bullet grazed her leg and I rendered her assistance."

Mrs. Lyman's lips narrowed into a harsh line. "That is my point, exactly. She spent last night with you in the cottage, without a chaperone."

"For mercy's sake, it was not her choice, nor mine! The lightning storm forced us to seek shelter."

Not at all mollified, Mrs. Lyman sucked in her cheeks and folded her arms across her chest. Logan sighed.

"Her aunt will collect her this afternoon," he said. "Can you bear with me until then?"

"The sooner she is gone, the better."

In a swirl of self-righteousness, Mrs. Lyman strode over to the door, yanked it open, and disappeared down the hall.

JILLIAN STIRRED awake when Mary brought in her traveling suit. The entrance and exit holes made by the bullet had been sewn shut, but not invisibly so. In addition, a faint brown streak remained on her petticoat and skirt—a stark reminder of her injury. Jillian lamented the ruination of a brand new suit, but was grateful she'd emerged from the misadventure so lightly.

The maid helped her dress and then brushed out her long locks.

"I've never seen hair this color before. It's near like snow," she said, awed.

"Oh, thank you. It's the same as my father's. He's Norwegian."

Mary arranged the hair into simple but elegant French twist. As the maid worked in the pins, Jillian examined her reflection in the mirror. Would The Upper Ten consider her pale coloring attractive? Mama used to tell her all the time how pretty she was…but that was when she was a little girl. Although Aunt Letty had assured her she would have no lack of suitors, because of her dowry, she wanted to marry for love. When her father used to look at her mother, the expression around his eyes would become softer and more vulnerable. Jillian vowed never to marry unless her suitor gazed at her like that.

A tap on the door interrupted her reverie.

"Come in," she said.

A rawboned young man stuck his head inside the room. "Excuse me, miss. My name is Tom, and I'm to take you to the library. The constable is here to speak with you."

"Oh, good." Jillian rose.

At her request, Tom set her down just inside the doorway of the library. The constable and Logan turned to meet her. A shock went down Jillian's spine at Logan's altered appearance. *Why, he's far younger than I had imagined.* The full beard was gone, revealing a very handsome face. His thick chestnut hair had been tamed, and he wore a black cutaway jacket that accentuated his broad shoulders. Jillian felt her cheeks grow warm and her heart beat faster. When Constable Bridges began to ask his questions, Logan moved out of her direct line of vision. Jillian was relieved. *Now I won't stammer my way through the interview.*

WHILE JILLIAN CONVERSED with the constable, Logan sat listening off to one side. As she spoke, he studied her face, mannerisms, and tone of address. *Mrs. Lyman is entirely mistaken to label the girl a trollop.* Jillian's conversation was cultivated, refined, and engaging. He'd thought her pretty from the moment he saw her, but now he fully appreciated how stunning she was. The girl's skin was poured cream and her cheeks bloomed with vitality. *She really is exquisite.* Logan caught himself staring at her lips and the slight cleft in her chin before tearing his gaze away. Those sorts of thoughts and feelings had been his undoing before, and he refused to entertain them now or in the future. *Neither Miss Roring nor her lips are of any consequence to me whatsoever.*

"Anyway, I'm horribly worried about my maid Betsy and her brother, George," Jillian was saying. "George suffered a gunshot wound and Betsy was terrified out of her wits. When the carriage stopped, she guessed immediately it was a highwayman."

"That's odd," interjected Logan. "Why would she be concerned about highwaymen? They aren't especially common anymore."

"I don't know, but she grew up in East End," Jillian said. "Perhaps she's more fearful of the criminal element than would ordinarily be the case."

"Miss Roring, were you carrying any valuables with you?" the constable asked.

"My handbag held several pound notes and coins, to pay our travel expenses, and my trunk was packed with clothes, footwear, and jewelry," she replied. "There was also the hatpin I used to defend myself. It was a gift from my father, Captain Roring, and I'm very sorry to lose it."

"Captain Lars Roring?" Logan asked, taken aback. "The Ice Captain?"

"The very same."

Constable Bridges's eyebrows rose. "Ice? Is he the one who imports Wenham Lake Ice from America? They say you can read a newspaper through a block of Wenham Lake Ice, but I've never tried it myself."

Jillian's blue eyes crinkled with merriment. "Most ice in Britain is imported from Norway these days. My father was born in Oslo."

"Is the good captain in England now?" the constable asked.

"His ship should be arriving at Regent's Canal Dock early in May, with his cargo."

The constable's notebook snapped closed and he stood. "I think I have enough to go on for the moment. If you'll excuse me, I have an investigation to conduct."

Jillian frowned. "I hope the brougham isn't in a ditch somewhere. The pistol shot startled the horses and George might not have been able to control them with one arm."

"Let me set your mind at ease. I assure you, there were no roadside accidents to be seen on my journey here today from Cirencester."

Constable Bridges bowed to Jillian and moved toward the door.

"I'll see you out, Constable," Logan said. "Excuse me, Miss Roring. I shall be back shortly. I believe Cook is prepared to serve lunch."

~

JILLIAN AND LOGAN dined on artichoke soup, chicken pie, fried broccoli, potatoes, and boiled beetroot. As the meal progressed, Logan's broody and reserved demeanor gave way to a far more relaxed attitude. He even exhibited a modicum of mischievous humor. *Under different circumstances, those Gypsy eyes of his would be a girl's undoing*, Jillian thought.

"What are your plans while you're in town, Miss Roring?"

"I'm to reside with my widowed aunt, Mrs. Leticia Marsh, in Eaton Square. That is, at least until the end of the Season."

"Of course."

"And you, sir? Will you be traveling to town?"

His spine stiffened and his expression turned hard. "No. I have no business in London, nor am I likely to in the future."

Although she was hurt by his abrupt response, Jillian pretended otherwise. She forced a smile to her lips. "You have such a beautiful home I can well understand your reluctance to leave it."

Had it been some dreadful occurrence in London that had changed him? Was that the awful news to which Aunt Letty had alluded? *Surely it's not gossip to wonder about the gentleman who rescued me?*

~

27

As soon as Logan spoke, he instantly regretted it. Miss Roring covered it well, but he could see a guarded look had appeared in her eyes. *Could you not have been more circumspect?* He cleared his throat and changed the subject.

"Were you born in England, Miss Roring?"

"Indeed, I was. My mother is originally from Nottingham. She met my father as a London debutante about twenty years ago. He was a dashing young Norwegian sea captain who'd made friends at the palace with the quality of his ice. Queen Victoria herself welcomed him to St. James."

"And where is your mother now?"

"She died giving birth to my stillborn brother when I was younger."

"I'm very sorry to hear it."

"Yes. I miss her terribly. I also wish I'd known my brother. My father was devastated. He's never been the same, really." Jillian paused. "The loss of one's mate is unusually difficult to bear, don't you agree?"

"I suppose so. My mother was inconsolable at first after my father passed, but then she adjusted tolerably well."

"I-I understand you yourself experienced a loss recently."

Logan was taken aback. "I beg your pardon?"

Two bright spots appeared on Jillian's cheekbones.

"I heard about the late Mrs. Logan and I assumed her passing was the reason for your melancholy."

A chill ran down his spine.

"That would be my mother, Miss Roring, and my *melancholy*, as you put it, is no concern of yours." He folded up his napkin, tucked it beside his plate, and stood. "If you'll excuse me, I seem to have lost my appetite."

He strode from the dining room.

IN THE WAKE of Logan's departure, Jillian stared at her plate in humiliation. She'd already imposed on the man, and now she'd insulted him. Not only that, but he also thought her a gossiping busybody. How would she ever move in society if she couldn't manage a civil conversation?

Moments later, Mrs. Lyman appeared. Her disapproving gaze swept the table, taking in Logan's half-finished meal and empty chair.

"Beg pardon, miss, but are you finished with lunch?"

Jillian struggled to her feet. "Yes, thank you."

With a sigh, she limped from the dining room and headed toward the staircase. She tried to climb the stairs, but discovered she would be unable to do so without dislodging the bandage around her wound. Truth be told, she had no desire to return to her room. Although it was impossible at present, she would have loved to go for a walk alongside the stream.

The open door of a library beckoned from across the hall, offering a temporary refuge. She peeked inside; the room seemed to be unoccupied. A gleaming black baby grand piano in the corner made her fingers itch with longing, but she didn't dare play it without permission. One note would probably send Mrs. Lyman running in with a broom. *Perhaps a book will help me pass a quiet afternoon.* A shelf of Dickens novels was close at hand. Since she was feeling a bit like an orphan herself, she chose *Oliver Twist*. The dark green leather binding was slightly worn, as if the book had been read many times.

She glanced around, trying to decide where to sit. Several high back wing chairs had been positioned around the room in small groupings. Had it been summertime, Jillian would have chosen a chair by the window. Because of the lingering springtime chill, however, she sat in the wing chair closest to the fire. Her eyes were drawn to the large portrait hung over the mantle. Mr. Mackenzie Logan stared down at her as he posed next to Tuxano. Jillian bit her lip as she imagined his disdain. The man was terribly handsome, but certainly scores of handsome men awaited her in London. Why should she care so much what Logan thought of her?

I don't care, not a jot.

After opening her book, she read the first line about the plight of poor baby Oliver. The second line became blurred, and then a teardrop fell on the page. Jillian hastily wiped the moisture away with her sleeve, but the tears continued to fall. With hiccupping sobs, she set aside the novel and fixed her swimming gaze on the glowing embers of the fire.

A rustling sound from across the room startled her. To her horror, Logan was crossing toward her, having been seated in the window-facing wingchair.

"Oh, no!" she gasped. "I can't seem to stop bothering you, can I?"

As he sank to one knee on the Persian rug, his expression was apologetic...and almost tender.

"You aren't a bother, Miss Roring."

He pressed his handkerchief into her hands. When his bare fingers accidentally brushed hers, she caught her breath.

"I apologize for my behavior," he said. "I should not have spoken to you the way I did at the table."

Her lips began to tremble. "I didn't mean to pry, Mr. Logan, especially in light of my inconvenient presence in your home."

"Our acquaintance may have begun in an unorthodox manner, but I enjoy your company. It *is* true I've been melancholy these past several months, but I believe you may have cheered me up a bit."

"Perhaps you should inform Mrs. Lyman. She doesn't seem to care for me."

"Yes, well...my housekeeper has the wrong idea about us, I'm afraid. I tried to dissuade her from the notion, but she's behaving in a beastly fashion all the same."

Jillian was appalled. "Does she imagine I shot myself in order to seduce you?"

"Mrs. Lyman has worked for my family since before I was born and has always had a rigid sense of propriety. Ever since the infamous sailor suit episode, she's been trying to cure me of my wicked ways."

His bended knee posture was in the manner of a suitor. Although Jillian's eyelashes were still damp, a mischievous giggle escaped her lips.

"If she were to walk in here this moment, she would have the wrong idea entirely."

He shook his head, puzzled, until a look of dawning comprehension crossed his features. In the next moment, he shot to his feet and straightened his clothes.

"I beg your pardon."

Her giggles were contagious, and Logan finally began to laugh. His gaze dropped to her book.

"Ah, I see you're reading Dickens. That's me as well. I was just re-reading *Great Expectations*."

"I love *Great Expectations*! What is your opinion of Estella? She is indeed wicked to lead Pip on so."

Logan sank into the wing chair next to Jillian.

"Perhaps, but her behavior has been inexorably shaped by Miss Havisham. Do you not think it sad Estella cannot admit her true feelings for Pip?"

"You give her far too much credit."

They slipped into easy conversation about the literary characters. At length, Logan was obliged to throw another log onto the fire.

A PROPOSAL

While George and Sam muscled the steamer trunk onto the train platform, Betsy sauntered ahead. She was dressed in a walking gown with a lacy shawl draped across her shoulders. Perched on her head sat a straw sailor's hat wrapped with a saucy red ribbon. Jillian's hatpin held it onto her brown curls. A quick diagonal step put her in the path of a well-heeled man in a top hat. As they nearly collided, Betsy put her gloved hands on his lapels.

"I'm so sorry," she murmured.

"Beg pardon, madam."

The man moved off just as the northbound train pulled into the station. Betsy slipped his purloined wallet into her reticule and took her place at the end of a queue waiting to board. She snapped her fingers at George and Sam.

"Come along."

A smirk lit her brother's face, but Sam gave Betsy a level look. Once on the train, the three entered a private compartment and slid the door closed. George and Sam lifted the trunk onto the storage shelf and then flopped down into their seats

SUZANNE G. ROGERS

with a sigh of relief. Betsy lowered herself grandly into her seat and tweaked the ends of her shawl.

"I don't much care fer the way yer treating me," Sam said. "I'm not yer lackey."

Betsy dropped her airs and clucked her tongue. "I don't hear my brother complainin'."

"That's 'cause ye've always treated me like a lackey," George said with a grin.

"And I'm not yer brother," Sam said.

"C'mon, Sam. I'm a lady now and as long as yer dressed like that, I have ter treat ye like my servant. When we get ter Liverpool, the both of ye need to behave like gentlemen and buy the proper clothes."

"But it takes money to get square rigged," Sam sputtered. "We hafta save every penny fer our passage!"

Betsy flipped the stolen wallet into Sam's lap. He gaped at the large number of pound notes inside. George hooted in amazement.

"She's got ye there, Sam!"

Despite himself, Sam grinned. He leaned over to bestow a kiss on Betsy's cheek. "There's my girl! If ye want a dandy by yer side, I can oblige."

"I've a hankering to pass for a gent meself," George said. He plucked the wallet from Sam's hand, counted out two-thirds of the bills, and tossed the wallet onto the seat. "I'll hold on ter my sister's take."

Betsy's fingers flew over toward the money in George's fist and peeled off several notes. "I'll hold on ter my own take, thank ye very much."

A long moment passed. Then George, Sam, and Betsy dissolved into laughter.

"Liverpool, here we come," George said.

"Nah, Georgie," Betsy said. "We're coming ter America."

S<small>IR</small> W<small>ILLIAM</small> and Aunt Letty arrived at Idunn Court at half-past four o'clock. Logan arranged for tea to be served in the library. While Jillian related her ordeal, Aunt Letty calmly sipped her tea. Sir William was far less composed, interjecting exclamations at the more exciting moments. Logan listened without comment, but he chuckled when Jillian described stabbing Sam with her hatpin.

"And so this morning, Mr. Logan brought me here to Idunn Court. He's been very kind and I'm in his debt," she finished.

Aunt Letty set down her teacup and saucer and exchanged a long meaningful glance with her elder brother. Far from the effusive thanks Jillian had expected, Sir William then gave Logan a hard stare. "I take it, sir, you do not intend to make my niece an offer of marriage?"

Both Jillian and Logan gasped.

"Uncle!" she exclaimed in horror. "Mr. Logan has given me no reason to anticipate an offer, nor have I sought one." She fixed her gaze on the carpet. From the burning of her cheeks, Jillian knew her face had grown as crimson as the roses woven into the pattern.

"I'm afraid you have caught me a bit off guard, sir," Logan managed.

"Mr. Logan, is there somewhere we can speak together privately?" Sir William asked.

"If you'll accompany me to my study, we may speak freely there."

As the two men left, Jillian gave her aunt a wounded look.

"How could Uncle William embarrass me so? I am completely humiliated!"

"Embarrassment is the least of your problems, child. Mr. Logan has a reputation as a rake."

"I…what does that have to do with me?"

"Do you not understand? Your chances to make a good marriage have been materially damaged by your intimate association with him." Aunt Letty said.

A protest spilled from Jillian's lips, but her aunt held up her hand to check it.

"The fact remains—you and he spent the night alone together."

"Not by choice!"

"However innocent you both may be, the situation is scandalous by anyone's reckoning."

"No one need know," Jillian said, a note of desperation in her voice. "I will not relate these matters to anyone and I feel certain Mr. Logan will keep my confidence!"

Aunt Letty shook her head and sighed. "Servants talk, Jillian, and even a hint of scandal will ruin your prospects. Let us hope William can reach an accord with Mr. Logan on your behalf."

"Let me be frank, Mr. Logan. Your failure to marry my niece may result in her downfall."

Logan stared at Sir William, aghast. "What? This is absurd!"

"I appeal to your sense as a gentleman, first and foremost. I can also assure you that it is a shrewd financial move on your part, since Jillian is the heiress to a large fortune."

"This is no reflection on Miss Roring, but I have forsworn marriage entirely!"

"Oh come now, sir. You cannot be more than five and twenty years old."

"I'm four and twenty this past March."

"At that age, whatever you feel at present will pass. Good heavens, man! Have you no eyes in your head? Jillian is a beautiful girl, very accomplished, and quite amiable. Your marriage to her will be seen as a coup by society."

"I care nothing for society!"

Sir William gave him a shrewd glance.

"I understand you once valued the opinion of Miss Sophia Watkins. The best revenge for a broken engagement is to marry well, Mr. Logan."

Logan flinched. "Revenge is beneath me, sir."

"Be that as it may."

WHILE THEY WERE ALONE, Aunt Letty told Jillian everything she'd heard about Logan's broken engagement.

"How sad. He must still be in love with her, I think," Jillian replied. She gazed at Logan's portrait. "It is impossible for me to understand how anyone would jilt the man."

A smile lifted the corners of Aunt Letty's mouth.

"You esteem him."

"Of course I esteem him! Who would not? He is quite gentlemanly."

"And handsome."

"Yes. He is the most handsome man ever seen."

"Idunn Court is comfortable and gracious too."

"I've rarely seen a more beautiful home, I grant you."

"Then as soon as William and Mr. Logan agree on the settlement, we shall plan a wedding."

Before Jillian could reply, her uncle and Logan reappeared. Although Logan appeared sober and withdrawn, Sir William's visage was wreathed with smiles.

"We are all in agreement," he said. He bestowed a kiss on Jillian's forehead. "Let me be the first to congratulate you on your engagement."

Jillian gasped and pulled herself up to her full height, ignoring the searing pain that followed.

"We are *not* in agreement, Uncle. I refuse to enter into an engagement with a man in love with someone else!"

"Have you lost your mind?" Aunt Letty exclaimed. "Love has nothing to do with marriage, on the whole."

"I...I have no objection, Miss Roring," Logan said.

Jillian gave him a searching look. "Forgive me, sir. Your offer is honorable, but motivated by obligation. I aspire to enter into more than an unobjectionable union."

"If these events between you and Mr. Logan become known, Jillian, this may be the only offer of marriage you will ever receive," Sir William said.

"So be it," Jillian said. "I will not marry unless the man has a true and abiding affection for me and I for him in return. My mind is made up on the matter and I won't discuss it further."

Aunt Letty's shrewd gaze moved from Logan to Jillian and back again.

"There's no other course open to us. My niece will return with me to London, and we shall all of us behave as if none of this ever happened. We will deny any acquaintance with you, Mr. Logan, and you with us. As for me, I shall lean upon my connections to ensure Jillian is married before this unfortunate event becomes public knowledge. I have every confidence she will make the match of the Season, if we play our cards right."

Aunt Letty rose from the sofa and gave Logan a regal nod. "Thank you, Mr. Logan, for your assistance to Jillian. We shall count on your discretion."

"You can be assured of my silence."

Sir William sighed and shook Logan's hand. "You are a gentleman, sir."

"Come along, Jillian, we've a train to catch," Aunt Letty said.

The woman sailed from the room, followed by her elder brother. Jillian took a step toward Logan.

"I am completely mortified, Mr. Logan," she murmured. "Know that I would not have chosen to discomfit you in this manner."

She curtsied and moved toward the door, trying desperately not to limp. In the doorway, she paused to glance back at Logan. As their eyes met, she gave him a tremulous smile. He bowed in return.

"Have a safe journey, Miss Roring. You'll need something to read on the train. Please allow me to give you my copy of *Great Expectations*."

Jillian paused a moment, then shook her head. "I thank you, sir, but I already know how it ends."

As she hastened to catch up to her aunt and uncle, she gulped back tears.

I shall never see him again.

THE CARRIAGE TOOK JILLIAN, Sir William, and Aunt Letty from Idunn Court to the train station in short order. After he ordered the driver to take the empty carriage back to his home in Gloucester, Sir William bought three tickets to Paddington Station.

"You're to come with us to town then?" Jillian asked.

"I'm going to make absolutely certain there's no more trouble...as I ought to have done in the first place."

"Don't blame yourself, Uncle. Nobody could have anticipated this," Jillian said.

"It's more my fault than my brother's," Aunt Letty said. "I should have insisted you stay with me in London after your presentation at court. Then we would have avoided this whole episode."

"If I ever get my hands around Sam Netherby's ungrateful neck, I'll wring it," Sir William said. "The maid was working with him, most certainly."

"That can't be true!" Jillian cried. "Betsy was fond of me."

"She was more fond of Sam, I'm afraid."

"What?"

"Oh, yes." Sir William nodded his head vigorously. "After I spoke with your aunt on the telephone earlier today, I asked a few discreet questions around the household. I discovered Betsy was sneaking out after hours to meet the scoundrel."

"My word! Do servant girls have no morality these days?" Aunt Letty exclaimed.

"If Betsy is implicated, so is her brother George," Sir William said.

Disappointment and shock washed over Jillian, but she was forced to admit her uncle's logic was sound.

"Perhaps you are right. After all, I never did see any blood. George might have been feigning injury. We must inform Constable Bridges. He's the one doing the investigation."

"You'll do no such thing, William," Aunt Letty said. "You must pay a visit to this constable and ask him to drop the investigation. Tell him we will not press charges."

"These thieves cannot be allowed to escape justice, Letty!" Sir William exclaimed.

"Is justice for petty criminals more important than Jillian's future? The fewer questions asked, the better."

AFTER HIS GUESTS HAD DEPARTED, Logan lingered in the library. He brought his book over to Jillian's chair and sat in front of the fire. When his attention wandered from the text, he put aside his book and paced the room instead. The events of the last two days had unfolded quite strangely. Miss Roring's romantic notions had fortunately saved him from an inconvenient marriage. Relief should be flowing through his veins...and yet he felt restless instead.

The unsettled feeling persisted through his solitary dinner of roast chicken, carrots, cucumber salad, and savory biscuits. As he drank a glass of port in his study afterward, his thoughts turned reluctantly to Miss Sophia Watkins.

Sophia.

The name had been as sweet as wine on his tongue nearly a year ago. Although the general opinion painted him as a rake, he did not deserve the label. He had the misfortune to be cornered by young, breathless debutantes attempting to secure him. He'd not stolen their kisses as much as they were pressed upon him. Then, when he chose not to deepen those fleeting acquaintances, he'd been accused of being a scoundrel. The accusations hadn't bothered him overmuch since he enjoyed being a bachelor. Then Sophia came along and changed everything.

For months he'd pursued her, and she'd warmed to his overtures. His proposal of marriage had been accepted for two glorious weeks. When the engagement was broken, London society ate up the scandal with extra delight. With nothing better to fill the void, his misery had furnished more than enough gossip to last the entire Season. Disgusted, he'd closed up his townhouse on Belgrave Square and left London, vowing never to marry.

With a frown, Logan poured himself another glass of port.

Despite that vow, however, he'd agreed to marry Miss Jillian Roring. Why? Had he done so to exact revenge on Sophia, as Sir William had suggested? No, the very idea was abhorrent. Jillian had brought out his protective instinct from the moment he saw her struggling with her kidnapper. Logan would have shot the man if he hadn't been afraid of hurting her in the process. Her shocked expression as she sat in the mud had been priceless. He chuckled at the recollection, but when he remembered kneeling at her feet earlier that afternoon, devastated by the knowledge he'd been the cause of her tears, his smile faded. The accidental touch of her hand had made him hunger for more. Oh, if only he'd met Jillian last Season, how different his life would be! He had not known her long, but he could tell she was not the sort of girl who would toy with his affections.

Blast it. I miss her already.

FRIENDS AND ACQUAINTANCES

*S*ir William, Jillian, and Aunt Letty debarked the train at Paddington station and hired a hansom cab to convey them to Aunt Letty's townhouse. Having brought no items of clothing with her, Jillian borrowed a nightdress from her aunt. The following morning, she was obliged to don one of her aunt's gowns. Although it was made of the finest materials, the dress was far too short in the hem and too loose in the waist.

After breakfast, Sir William summoned a cab to take him to the train station. He promised to stop in Cirencester on the way home, to dissuade Constable Bridges from pursuing his investigation.

"Good-bye, Letty. Good-bye, Jillian. May you successfully excite dozens of well-heeled, handsome gentlemen to propose," he said.

She giggled. "One will do, if he truly cared for me. Can't you stay awhile? Papa will be in town the first week of May."

"You are quite welcome to stay, Brother," Aunt Letty said. "We could use a male opinion on Jillian's new wardrobe."

"Thank you, no." He shuddered. "Discussions of satin, tulle, and lace make me itch. I would only be in the way. Send me the bills and I shall participate by making sure they are paid promptly."

After Sir William had departed. Jillian turned to her aunt.

"What shall we do today? I should love to go sight-seeing."

"That will have to wait. First, we must build you a brand-new wardrobe from scratch."

Jillian stifled a giggle. "How dreadful."

Aunt Letty's usual reserve gave way to a smile.

"All right, my girl, perhaps there are worse things than shopping for clothes, but you're not fit to be seen in public in a borrowed dress. Not only that, but you need time for your limp to improve. We don't want anyone thinking you were born with a clubfoot. What's worse, we have engagements to attend within the month. *Tempus fugit!*" She headed for the telephone. "It's a good thing I have connections."

IN HIS SHIRTSLEEVES, Logan leaned over the pool table with his cue and banked a shot off the rail. Although he sank the ball he sighed. Mrs. Lyman appeared in the doorway of the game room.

"Excuse me, sir, but Mr. Hawkins has come to call."

The news lightened Logan's mood.

"Show him in please."

Mr. Andrew Hawkins entered the room moments later with a broad smile on his handsome face. He and Logan exchanged a hearty handshake.

"Hello, Hawkins!"

"Hello, Logan! I nearly fell off my horse when I heard you'd come back to Idunn Court. I've missed your company."

"And I yours. You look well."

"As do you, except you seem a trifle thin."

Logan handed his friend a pool cue. "Not as slender as your hopes of winning at billiards. Are you up for a game or two?"

"Ha!" Hawkins set down the cue long enough to shrug off his cutaway. "You *must* be feeling better if you're in the mood for a trouncing."

The two men spent a pleasant morning in a lighthearted competition to best one another at pool. When the score was even, however, Hawkins lay down his cue.

"I'm afraid I must go, Logan. I am preparing to go to town tomorrow for the Season." He paused. "If you say you'll travel with me, however, I'll gladly delay my departure."

"No, I'm done with all that. I'm a confirmed bachelor now."

"Come now, Logan. It's time to get back on the horse, as it were. London won't be nearly as much fun without you."

"I'll think of you often and wish you much success in evading the Ogleby girls."

Hawkins slipped into his coat and shook his head, resignedly. "Mrs. Ogleby is quite determined to extract my proposal to one of her daughters, but I am equally determined to withhold it. Nevertheless, I wouldn't mind seeing Miss Heathrow again, nor Miss Fairley. Logan, it would help me pluck up my courage if you were there to cheer me on."

"I'll be there in spirit, I assure you." Logan shook his friend's hand in farewell. "It was good seeing you."

Hawkins studied Logan, perplexed. "Dash it all, I wish you'd change your mind. Give me a ring if you do. I just had a telephone put in, and nobody ever calls me!"

The gentleman left, taking his warmth and good cheer with him. Logan sighed as he re-racked the balls. Mrs. Lyman entered the room.

"Excuse me, sir, but luncheon is served."

"I'm not hungry, Mrs. Lyman."

To his surprise, the housekeeper remained where she was.

"Was there something else?" he asked.

"I spoke out of turn yesterday."

His eyebrows lifted. "About what?"

"Miss Roring. Her relatives are respectable gentlefolk."

"Yes, they are."

"I shouldn't have called her a trollop."

"No, you shouldn't have done."

"I'm sorry, and I thought you ought to know."

"Thank you, Mrs. Lyman." He paused. "Have Tom saddle up Tuxano for me, please. I'm going to ride over to the hunting cottage for a few days."

"That's what you said last time and you were gone for months."

"That will be all, Mrs. Lyman."

The housekeeper refused to budge. "Why don't you go to town with Mr. Hawkins? He's a proper gentleman and always good company."

"You overheard our conversation?"

"There's not much I don't hear in this house." She frowned, arms akimbo. "I *won't* let you hide away another three months!"

Logan was taken aback. "Mrs. Lyman, have you been drinking?"

"For the few hours Miss Roring was here, you seemed your normal self."

Logan shrugged as he rolled the cue ball back and forth with his fingers. "That's beside the point."

"You need the society of young people. Go to town, visit your gentleman's clubs, and pay a few calls," Mrs. Lyman said. "Invitations will begin to arrive."

"Why ever would I want to do that?"

"Because if you don't, you'll have no peace from me!"

Logan peered at Mrs. Lyman. "You are quite determined?"

"No peace at all."

Her presumptuousness would ordinarily have annoyed

Logan, but instead he was unaccountably amused. A crooked grin crept onto his face.

"All right. Send some of the staff on ahead to prepare my townhouse, and direct Ian to pack my trunks. I'll call Hawkins."

AUNT LETTY'S townhouse was a whirlwind of activity. Milliners, seamstresses, and couturiers came and went in a flurry of tape measures, swatches of fabric, ribbons, trims, and finishings. Jillian quickly realized London fashion was so *au courant* her old wardrobe would have not been up to the task in any case. Under Aunt Letty's eagle-eyed supervision, she was fitted for dozens of walking dresses, riding costumes, afternoon dresses, tea gowns, evening gowns, dinner gowns, and ball gowns, in such fabrics as silk, satin, moiré, velvet, chiffon, peau de soie, and cashmere. As it was spring, Aunt Letty also ordered a variety of lightweight capes, mantles, coatlets, and Victorines with high fluted collars for nighttime. Undergarments, such as petticoats, chemises, and knickers were given equal attention. Jillian was relieved to find tight laces were no longer required, and she delighted in the newer skeleton corsets trimmed in pretty ribbons and lace.

"But, Aunt, what of hats? We've not purchased nearly enough to go with all my new clothes," Jillian said.

"That's on purpose. Shopping at most fashionable milliners on Bond and Regent Streets will allow you to mix with titled and powerful ladies. We have yet to shop for accessories or jewelry, either."

"I had not thought of that."

"Which is why you have me to guide you. Trust me, my dear, you have many natural gifts in your favor. Your feet are far too large, but there is less emphasis on a small foot now than there used to be. Just keep them tucked away whenever you can. On the positive side, your face is lovely, and your hair is the most remarkable color. No bust improvers will be necessary for you or padding for your hips. Your face and figure will be much admired, but you must pretend not to notice."

"'Tis a blessing Uncle William isn't here. With all this talk of clothes, I'm afraid he would have taken to his bed with a painful rash!"

Aunt Letty laughed. "When he receives the bills, he will."

"Do you suppose we could tour London? I'd dearly love to see the palace again and—"

"None of your gowns are ready yet! You cannot leave the house until you look absolutely perfect."

"But—"

"Of this much you can be sure; London society talks amongst themselves, and not all of the conversation is laced with Christian charity. As soon as you have a suitable afternoon dress delivered, we shall call on my dear friend, Lady Fanny Adams. She knows simply everyone."

In the meantime, Aunt Letty's extensive collection of penny dreadfuls provided Jillian with a pleasant diversion, as did the upright piano in the parlor. Jillian practiced melancholy sonatas until Aunt Letty finally put her foot down.

"Dearest, there's some brand-new sheet music in the bench from *The Pirates of Penzance* and *The Mikado*. Play something cheerful for a while so the cook doesn't curdle the soup."

Lacking any bosom friends to talk to, Jillian also began a diary. As she sat in the parlor, she poured out in its pages her misadventure with Sam Netherby, her interactions with Mr. Logan at Idunn Court, and her subsequent journey by train to town:

I must conclude this entry with a confession, Dear Diary. Mr. Logan stirs within me feelings I cannot begin to comprehend. I must seek another upon whom to attach my affections, however, lest I fall prey to the same melancholy that afflicts Mr. Logan at the perfidy of Miss Sophia Watkins.

~

BETSY FLOUNCED over to the bed and sat down. A cloud of dust set her coughing. The sound of a baby crying in the next room made her want to plug her ears. The smells seeping through the floorboards were worse. Rather than sit in the rickety chair next to the bed, George chose to sit on Betsy's trunk instead. Oblivious, Sam strode toward the window and looked outside.

"Why are we stayin' here, Sam?" Betsy asked. "I want ter stay in a nice place and be treated like a lady."

"Aye, Sam, this is a bit rough, don't ye think?" George added. "This must be the worst Nethersken in Liverpool."

"Shut it. I asked the cabbie ter find us lodgings what is reasonable," Sam replied. "Here on Scottie Road, we blend in, as it were."

"I don't blend in! Not dressed like this, anyhow," Betsy said.

Without warning, Sam leaned over and snatched off one of her gold earbobs. She gasped in pain. "That hurt!" When he reached for the other earbob, Betsy knocked his hand away. "Leave off!"

Sam drew his arm back, as if to slap her. George shot to his feet, his fists clenched. "Oi, what do ye think yer doing ter my sister?"

"I'm taking these luggers to a dollyshop ter sell. I thought we all agreed."

"Only if we ran out of money," Betsy wailed, tears spilling down her face. "And ye could have asked me. That earbob was screwed on tight."

Her fingers touched her injured earlobe and came away bloody.

George's voice was low. "Ye manhandle my sister like that again mate, you'll be the one bleedin'."

Sam bristled a moment before glancing away.

"The devil take the both of ye. Gimme the other one, quick like."

Distraught, Betsy unscrewed the other earbob and practically threw it at Sam. Unperturbed, he pocketed the earbobs and headed for the door.

"I'm thirsty. I'm going out ter find a lush."

Betsy shot to her feet. "Sam?"

"Yeah?"

She rushed over to give him a hug. "Don't be mad at me, Sam. I love ye."

"Yeah, all right."

He slammed out of the room. After a moment, Betsy sighed and wiped her tears away. "All he cares about is drinkin'."

George patted her on the back. "Are ye beginnin' to think maybe Sam don't really love ye?"

With a bitter laugh, Betsy opened her hand to reveal the gold earbobs. "Sam can go to blazes. Let's go find ourselves a ship."

THE TAVERN WAS DARK, dirty, and anonymous. Sam peered at his hand of cards, knocked back another tot of Irish whisky, and pushed his money into the pot. He laid down his cards, faces up. "I got ten. Ha!"

"I gots me eleven, mate," said the swarthy man on his right.

"Bloody hell. Ye've got the luck o' the devil himself!" Sam exclaimed.

The man peered at Sam with narrowed eyes. "Ye wouldn't be accusin' me of cheatin', would ye?"

Sam combed back his greasy hair with fingers numb from drink. "'Course not."

The burly man to his left folded his massive arms across his muscular chest.

"Yer outta money, friend. Time fer ye ter get home ter the missus with yer tail between yer legs."

"And best pray she don't slit yer throat," said the third player.

Everyone but Sam burst into raucous, mocking laughter.

"I got me some luggers worth a bit o' money," he said, patting his pocket. "Let's play."

"Show 'em or get out."

A bewildered expression came over Sam's face when he realized the earbobs were missing. With increasing panic, he checked his other pockets.

"I-I musta left 'em in the room."

The bartender stood over Sam, arms akimbo. "Did ye say yer out of money? How're ye goin' ter settle yer tab?"

Sam lurched to his feet. "I'm good fer it, I tell ye!"

Moments later, he found himself flying through the door of the tavern by the seat of his pants. He landed in the cobblestone street, onto a pile of horse droppings left from earlier in the day. Cursing and railing, he picked himself up and staggered down the street toward the boarding house.

The glimmer of dawn was creeping through the dirty window when he opened the door to his room. To his dismay, Betsy and George were missing. Worse, the steamer trunk was gone, and the bed had not been slept in. Sam kicked a hole through the wall. In the next room, the baby woke up from the noise and began to scream.

CLAD IN HER NEW FINERY, Jillian settled herself in the Victoria carriage next to her aunt. A pastel blue afternoon dress hugged her body around the hips and then flared out where the stitched-down pleats ended. The fluted collar of a bolero-style jacket framed her face. On her carefully arranged hair rested a halo hat with a curving white plume.

"Phelps, we are calling on Lady Fanny Adams, on Park Lane," Aunt Letty called out to the coachman.

"Yes, madam."

"This beautiful spring weather is absolutely perfect for a carriage ride. Let's do take the long way 'round, Aunt," Jillian urged. "I want to see absolutely everything in London!"

"We haven't time to canvas all of London today, but a little detour can't do any harm," Aunt Letty said. "Phelps, drive past Buckingham Palace before you circle around to Park Lane."

"As you like, madam."

A beatific smile lit Jillian's face. As the carriage moved along Eaton Square, she marveled at the long line of townhouses. Aunt Letty kept up a running narrative, pointing out landmarks and houses where her friends lived. To Jillian's delight, she also related a few ongoing scandals involving prominent members of society.

Buckingham Palace was little over a half mile from her aunt's home. As the gig drove past the edifice, Jillian leaned forward to drink in the view.

"It's like a great big wonderful present, isn't it?" Jillian exclaimed.

"Buckingham Palace is a lovely sight, I'll grant you."

After they passed the palace, they drove along Constitution Hill. Jillian enjoyed the tree-lined street, with its view toward Wellington Arch. Many fashionable matrons were out for a stroll, parasols in hand. A little further on, the carriage turned onto Park Lane. Aunt Letty pointed out the Grosvenor House.

"That home was one of the first buildings in London to have electricity," she said. "The wide-spread use of electricity is short-sighted, in my opinion. Ladies are always far more attractive under gaslight."

Jillian giggled as she laced her arm through her aunt's. "Thank you."

"What are you thanking me for?"

"For all this. Mama would be so grateful to you for sponsoring me this Season. When it's over, I can go back home to Gloucester quite contented."

"You shall not leave London without being married. I simply forbid it."

"Do you think I can induce someone to fall in love with me in a few short months?"

"You will take the gentlemen of London society by storm."

"From what I've heard, they are already smitten with Miss Sophia Watkins."

"Although I don't know the whole of the affair between her and Mr. Logan, I believe his humiliation was quite complete. It was quite a downfall, since he was much pursued himself."

"So *that* is why he refuses to come to London. I cannot think why she broke the engagement, unless it was to prolong her time in the limelight."

"Do not be so quick to judge Miss Watkins, Jillian. Neither of us is privy to the particulars."

"You are quite right, Aunt Letty."

But I am already inclined to despise her.

THE HOME of Lady Fanny Adams, while not as magnificent as the Grosvenor House, was luxurious nevertheless. The three-story mansion was of Grecian design. Fluted columns supported a balcony overlooking Hyde Park. A butler showed Jillian and her aunt into an elegant drawing room where his mistress was receiving visitors. Lady Adams greeted Aunt Letty warmly and bestowed a kiss on her cheek. The woman's bright eyes fell upon Jillian next.

"And this must be the niece you've been telling me about?"

"Yes, indeed. Fanny, this is Miss Jillian Roring. Jillian, let me introduce you to Lady Adams."

Jillian and Lady Adams curtsied to one another. Jillian was pleased to discover her wound no longer pained her overmuch.

"Please do sit down, Letty and Miss Roring," Lady Adams said.

Lady Adams chose a floral pattern armchair upon which to perch, while Aunt Letty and Jillian sank down onto a Rococo sofa with damask upholstery. At the last moment, Jillian remembered to slide her feet back under her skirt until not even the pointed tips were showing.

"Tell me, Miss Roring, how do you find London?"

The next few minutes were filled with seemingly idle chatter. Jillian had the distinct feeling, however, Lady Adams was subtly extracting bits of useful information. Within a short period of time, Lady Adams discovered Jillian spoke French, played the piano, sang a little, had learned how to shoot with Uncle William, and rode for pleasure but had never ridden to hounds.

"And your father, my dear? Will I have the pleasure of seeing him?"

"Yes, ma'am. His ship should be arriving in a fortnight."

"You should have received an invitation to my ball by now. Please bring Captain Roring with you, if he's not otherwise engaged."

"That's very kind of you, Lady Adams," Jillian said.

Aunt Letty kept uncharacteristically quiet during the visit, but when the butler entered the drawing room carrying another calling card on a silver salver, she stood.

"You have another visitor, Fanny. We really must be going."

Lady Adams read the name on the calling card and smiled. "Oh, stay just a little while longer, Letty. I'd like to introduce you and Miss Roring to my friends."

The butler thereafter ushered in a handsome older woman and well-dressed girl about Jillian's age. The young lady was an absolutely stunning brunette, with dazzling hazel eyes framed by well-defined eyebrows.

"I don't mean to intrude, Lady Adams," the woman said. "I see you already have callers."

"Letty and Miss Roring, before you leave, allow me to introduce my friends Mrs. Watkins and her daughter, Miss Watkins. Mrs. Watkins and Miss Watkins, this is my good friend Mrs. Marsh and her niece, Miss Roring."

Mrs. Watkins nodded at Aunt Letty, but her gaze cooled considerably when her eyes locked onto Jillian. "Miss Roring."

Jillian was taken aback. The older woman's words seemed less a greeting and more a statement of fact. She forced herself to smile.

"Pleased to meet you, Mrs. Watkins."

"I believe Miss Roring and Miss Watkins just may be the belles of the Season," Lady Adams said.

Miss Watkins studied Jillian for a long moment before a smile graced her perfect lips. Her next words confirmed Jillian's worst suspicions.

"I think we should be good friends. Do call me Sophia."

ON THE RIDE HOME, Jillian gazed at the scenery without comment. Her muted demeanor did not escape her aunt's notice.

"You did not have to agree to go riding with Miss Watkins tomorrow afternoon, you know," Aunt Letty said.

"Yes, but if I had declined, it would have seemed odd. Since Lady Adams offered us the use of her stables, I did not wish to appear ungrateful."

"Oh, I agree you've acted prudently, but I don't like to see you unhappy."

"Forgive me, Aunt Letty. I'm not at all unhappy. It's just that my meeting with Miss Watkins—Sophia—was unexpected."

"And not entirely welcome."

"Exactly. I did not expect her to be quite so beautiful, nor so congenial."

"I would certainly be on my guard with Miss Watkins if I were you," Aunt Letty said. "At this point, her motives are unclear."

"True. And although I am inclined to think ill of Miss Watkins, perhaps our deeper acquaintance will absolve her of blame in her dealings with Mr. Logan."

Or perhaps I will convict her more firmly.

A TOAST TO MISS RORING

*A*top her borrowed pony, Jillian surveyed the broad riding path in Hyde Park known as Rotten Row. The long straight track was filled with groups or pairs of riders in fashionable apparel. Clad in her brand-new riding habit of lightweight navy wool, Jillian was genuinely elated to partake of an activity traditionally favored by London society—despite her unfortunate riding companion. Sophia was similarly dressed, but her habit was an eye-catching deep periwinkle blue.

"I know you want to gossip, so you may ride on ahead a bit, girls," Mrs. Watkins said.

"Thank you, Mama," Sophia said.

"Thank you, Mrs. Watkins," Jillian echoed.

Atop her mare, Mrs. Watkins kept a discreet distance behind as Sophia and Jillian guided their mounts onto the sandy track. Sophia set the pace at a little more than a walk.

"Why on Earth is this place called Rotten Row?" Jillian asked.

"It's a bit of a joke. About two hundred years ago it was called *Route de Roi* and the name evolved over time."

"Kings Road," Jillian translated.

"Ah, you speak French." Sophia paused. "Have you been presented at court?"

"I was presented before Easter. I met Her Majesty one other time, in a manner of speaking. My father, Captain Roring, is a favorite of hers. He took me to the palace when I was a baby."

Sophia laughed. "What a precious story. I was presented at court last spring. I wore an exquisite gown with a ten-foot train. Her Majesty even remarked on my looks. Isn't that lovely?"

"What a wonderful honor!"

"Your papa...he's the Ice Captain, is he not?"

Jillian smiled. The nickname never failed to delight her. "Yes."

"You might not want to mention that to anyone else."

"Why not?"

Sophia wrinkled her pert nose. "I'm sure he's a very good sort of man but importing ice is an awful lot like being in trade."

Shocked, Jillian didn't know how to respond. Sophia mistook her expression for fear.

"Oh, don't worry. We're friends, so your secret is safe with me."

"I thank you, truly, but I don't have anything to conceal as far as my father is concerned."

Sophie gave Jillian a pretty little pout, as if she were a small child who'd just been caught doing something naughty. "Please don't be vexed with me. Mama says I blurt out truths in an unvarnished fashion and it's frightfully rude. For example, may I tell you I'm terribly envious of your hair? You've the appearance of an angel. Your coloring and mine are quite the opposite of one another. We're marvelously balanced."

"You flatter me. I can't imagine you being envious of anything."

A delicate peal of laughter bubbled up from Sophia's throat. "Can you not? I *knew* you were amiable."

LOGAN AND HAWKINS had donned their best clothes for Rotten Row. Logan was astride glossy and sleek Tuxano, while Hawkins rode a handsome chestnut quarter horse.

"Hawkins, when you said I should get back on the horse, you meant it literally, didn't you?" Logan chuckled.

"Leaving our calling cards everywhere won't be enough. We must be seen out and about, Logan. You must quash the rumors of your broken heart."

"And you must allay fears that you became engaged over the winter."

As he spoke, the image of Miss Roring flashed into Logan's mind. Hawkins had no idea how close *he'd* come to being engaged recently. Not even the greatest affection for his friend, however, would induce Logan to confess it. If he wanted to claim an acquaintance with Miss Roring, he would have to seek a proper introduction through mutual friends—the more highly placed, the better. The challenge would be to find a mutual friend willing to introduce him.

Logan and Hawkins trotted along the track, pausing frequently to greet persons they knew. All of the young ladies sat up straighter in their sidesaddles when Logan approached. The girls sent appreciative glances and dazzling smiles his way, until their chaperones shooed their charges along. Hawkins was not without admirers. To his dismay, the three Ogleby sisters rode their matched trio of Palomino ponies across his path, along with their ambitious mother. Logan laughed inwardly as he waited for Hawkins to artfully fend off a naked solicitation to call at the Ogleby household the following afternoon.

Tuxano pawed the sand beneath his hooves and tossed his head as another pair of female riders drew close. Logan glanced over, and his stomach dropped. Miss Sophia Watkins was gazing at him as if she were a beautiful, spoiled cat contemplating a bowl of cream. Worse, she was in the company of Miss Roring.

JILLIAN'S HEART began to pound long before Logan happened to see her. From many yards away, his broad shoulders and athletic frame could perhaps be mistaken for someone else—but his mount Tuxano could not. *What is Mr. Logan doing here? I thought he'd foresworn society altogether.* When Sophia directed her mount toward Tuxano, Jillian had little choice but to follow.

As they approached, Logan lifted his hat in greeting.

"Good afternoon, Miss Watkins."

"Good afternoon, Mr. Logan," Sophia replied.

When Logan's eyes slid past Sophia and locked onto Jillian, a surge of pleasure ran down her spine. She fought to keep her countenance. *I must not appear to know him.*

"Jillian, allow me to introduce Mr. Logan to you. Mr. Logan, this is my friend, Miss Roring."

"It's a pleasure to make your acquaintance, Miss Roring."

"Thank you, Mr. Logan," Jillian replied.

"Have you been in town long, sir?" Sophia asked.

"Since yesterday. I expect you are looking forward to the delights of the Season?"

"Indeed I am, as is Miss Roring."

A fair-haired gentleman on a chestnut stallion joined Logan at that moment.

"Miss Watkins! What a pleasant surprise."

"Thank you, Mr. Hawkins."

Sophia introduced Jillian to Hawkins, whose merry smile invited one of her own.

"It's a pleasure, sir," Jillian said.

Although both men were very handsome, the differences between the two were marked. Hawkins was instantly congenial and friendly whereas Logan was somewhat broody and reserved. Yet Jillian found her eyes drawn inexorably to Logan, almost like a flower reaching toward the sun.

"Tell me, Miss Roring, why have I never happened to see you before?" Hawkins asked.

"I was raised in Gloucester."

"Why that's not terribly far from my estate in the Cotswolds! Logan and I are neighbors, in fact."

Logan cleared his throat. "Perhaps—"

But Mrs. Watkins rode up then, and whatever Logan had been meaning to say was lost in another round of greetings, pleasantries, and then farewells. Although etiquette demanded Jillian not look back after she'd ridden on, she could not help stealing the briefest of glimpses. Logan was watching as she rode away—or was he watching Sophia?

HAWKINS GAVE LOGAN A SYMPATHETIC SMILE. "That was unfortunate, meeting Miss Watkins so soon."

"Perhaps since I was dreading it, it was for the best. At least it's over now."

"Her friend Miss Roring is very striking indeed."

"If you intend to woo her along with Miss Fairley and Miss Heathrow, you will be quite busy."

"If I didn't know better, I would say your voice had a bit of an edge just now. Might I detect some interest in the girl yourself?"

"No. I've already told you I intend to remain unmarried."

Hawkins chortled. "I don't believe that."

"As you like."

"All is fair in love and war, my friend. I say we both throw our hats into the ring and see which one of us the young lady prefers."

"Miss Roring is hardly a game of billiards!"

"You should hope not. Otherwise, you will lose. Besides which, it's bad luck for you she's a good friend of Miss Watkins."

"Miss Roring cannot be a particular friend of Miss Watkins if she is just arrived to town. Besides which, since it was Miss Watkins who broke off our engagement, she can have nothing ill to say about my behavior to poison the well."

JILLIAN'S FEELINGS were tied in knots. What had brought Logan back to London, after he claimed he had no business here? His expression and manner upon their meeting had given her no clue whatsoever. *Perhaps he wishes to renew his offer to Sophia after all. If so, she does not deserve him.*

Sophia urged her pony closer to Jillian's, so their conversation could not easily be overheard. "I was engaged to Mr. Logan briefly, last Season."

Jillian feigned surprise. "Were you?"

"Mr. Logan is a heartless, incorrigible rake."

Started, Jillian gave Sophia a sharp look. "I don't know him at all, of course, but he appears to be gentlemanly."

"Appearances don't always tell the whole story. I would ordinarily say nothing, but since you seem quite taken with him, I would not be a good friend if I didn't warn you." Jillian felt her face grow hot. "If my behavior just now indicated I was taken with Mr. Logan, I am mortified!"

"Oh, it was obvious only to me, I assure you."

Jillian and Sophia rode on for a few moments in silence.

"Well...what leads you to say Mr. Logan is a rake?" Jillian asked finally.

"See? I knew you were taken with him."

"I am *not* taken with him! We've only just met!"

"Mr. Logan seizes every opportunity to maneuver pretty girls into dark corners and empty rooms to take liberties with them."

In response, Jillian gasped. "No!"

"And *that* is why I broke our engagement."

Jillian's hands trembled. Could Sophia be speaking the truth? "I-I'm...shocked."

"Any girl wed to Mr. Logan can expect to have a loveless marriage."

"Surely not."

"Which is why I mean to secure him as soon as possible."

Jillian gulped. "What did you say?"

"I've had a change of heart. Since I refused Mr. Logan, I've had months to contemplate my future. I finally realized love has nothing to do with marriage."

"That's what my aunt says, too."

"You sound disappointed."

"It's just that, well, I mean to marry for love."

"Then for pity's sake, steer clear of Mr. Logan before he sullies your reputation. A misstep would prove fatal to your chances to make a good match."

"But *you* mean to marry him, Sophia. What of *your* reputation?"

"My reputation is well guarded. You, my dear friend, are a new, fresh face. Mrs. Adams told me of your background. Although you have a vast fortune, you've no powerful connections to recommend you."

"My mother was the daughter of a gentleman!"

"Oh, you're a dear sweet thing, aren't you? *Every* girl who circulates in society is at least the daughter of a gentleman."

"M-My uncle has been knighted."

Sophia gave her a sidelong glance. "Oh, Jillian, I could throw a rock and hit half a dozen gentlemen of the knighthood right now." She paused. "I give you leave to like Mr. Hawkins. Of him, I have nothing ill to say."

Speechless, Jillian stared straight ahead. She'd begun her ride on Rotten Row cheerful and joyous. Now, however, she felt belittled and insignificant. Preoccupied and unsettled, the remainder of the afternoon's ride flew by in a blur. Sophia introduced her to several more gentlemen and a score of ladies, but a sudden, lancing headache made it difficult for Jillian to remember every name.

Sophia's accusation toward Logan disturbed her more than she cared to admit. The man had always acted in a gentle-manly manner in Jillian's presence, but the fact of the broken engagement seemed to support Sophia's assertion. Jillian thought back to that moment in the Idunn Court library when his hand had brushed hers. If Logan had leaned in to kiss her just then, she would have let him. No, she would have *welcomed* it—but he had not. Yet according to Sophia, he'd been claiming kisses freely all over London. Jillian could only conclude Logan did not find her attractive enough to bother. Perhaps next to Sophia's vibrant beauty, she suffered by comparison.

So Mr. Logan, with his wicked Gypsy eyes, is fond of ruining repu-tations is he? He may deserve Sophia after all.

AFTER DEBATING whether or not to dine that evening at The Athenaeum or Boodle's, Logan and Hawkins wound up at White's. While relaxing after dinner with a brandy, Logan suffered through some good-natured ribbing from his circle of friends about his broken engagement.

"It's well and good you've come back to town, Logan," said Lord Yardley. "Watching the ladies vie for your attention has always been amusing. Now that you're available again, this Season should be the most contentious ever."

Sir James laughed. "Having Miss Watkins slip through your fingers was a hard blow indeed. You must score a triumph to reclaim your dignity."

"I know just the thing!" Nelson exclaimed. "I happened across Miss Watkins as she was riding on Rotten Row this afternoon. She had a most beautiful companion...whose name I cannot now recall."

"Miss Roring," Hawkins supplied.

"That's it!" Nelson said. "Whoever manages to win *her* favor will be a fortunate man indeed."

"Yes, I met her today as well," Sir James said. "I was instantly smitten."

"As was I," Hawkins said. "I believe Miss Roring may be sweet Bianca to Miss Watkins's Katherina."

"If you wish to set Logan on her, Nelson, I'm afraid he will have some competition from me!" Sir James said.

"And me," Hawkins said.

"What good sport!" exclaimed Nelson. "Even money on Logan."

Logan frowned. "Now see here! I refuse to be part of any wager where Miss Roring is concerned."

Sir James gave Logan a sly glance. "Has Miss Watkins turned our prize stallion into a gelding?"

Boisterous laughter, lubricated by wine and spirits, filled the room.

"Not in the least," Logan said when the din ebbed. "It just that Miss Roring is a lady worth more than any wager."

"Oh, ho! You speak as if you know her, Logan. Is she a woman of title or property?" Sir James asked.

"My introduction to Miss Roring today was brief, as Hawkins will attest," Logan said. "As to her lineage or property, I cannot speak." *Or rather, I will not speak.*

"Dash it all," Sir James said.

"What are you going on about, Sir James?" Hawkins said.
"Since you have both lineage and property, you can afford to marry for less material considerations."

"True, but there's the additional question of the girl's reputation," Sir James replied.

"It will all come out in due course, but Miss Roring seems quite properly demure," Hawkins said.

Nelson raised his glass in a toast. "Gentlemen, I sense a competition heating up. Here's to the courtship of Miss Roring...May the best chap prevail!"

As their friends and acquaintances drank, Logan and Hawkins exchanged a rueful glance.

"What did I say to provoke such rivalry?" Logan asked.

"You waved a red flag in front of a field of bulls, I'm afraid," Hawkins replied.

"Blast it."

GEORGE EMERGED from the Red Star Line ticket office and headed down the wharf with his hands stuffed in his pockets. Frustrated, he kicked at a pebble. How was he going to break the news to his sister they couldn't leave for America until July? Worse, how were they to pay for their lodgings at that fancy bed and breakfast for two more months? They'd just have to sell those gold earbobs and hatpin Betsy had been so jealously guarding.

When he reached the sidewalk, George glanced over to discover Sam Netherby was walking straight toward him. As if George had shouted out his name, Sam's head jerked up. When he recognized George, Sam's eyes widened, and then narrowed in anger.

"Oh, *bollocks!*" George muttered.

He darted across the street with Sam in pursuit. As he ducked into an alley, he narrowly missed a horse and carriage rolling past. Fortunately, the rig delayed Sam long enough for George to make a clean getaway. He zigzagged his way south and west for fifteen minutes until he was sure he'd lost Sam altogether. Breathing hard, George slowed into a stroll, wiped his brow, and straightened his new clothes. He'd reached a nicer part of Liverpool and didn't want to be stopped by coppers or mistaken for a scoundrel.

Betsy was sitting next to the window, knitting, when he entered their room. A look of anxiety crossed her face when she saw his disheveled state.

"What's wrong?"

George tossed his bowler hat onto the bed and flopped into a chair.

"I saw Sam."

She gasped. "What happened?"

"I ran, of course. I don't think he trailed me here, but he won't stop scourin' Liverpool until he finds us."

"Did ye get the tickets?"

"There's nothin' but first class tickets left on the *S/S Belgenland*, Betsy. We can't afford two, and the next ship won't leave till July."

Betsy's eyes filled with tears.

"Now, lass, let's have none of that." He leaned forward. "Here's what we're goin' ter do. I'm goin' back ter the ticket office and buy ye first class passage to Philadelphia. The ship leaves in a few days and we can hide from Sam until then."

"But, George, what about ye?"

"Ach, I'd only weigh ye down, Betsy. Here ye are, lookin' all fine, like a real lady. Even in this new suit, I can't pass for a flash toff."

"Georgie, we were goin' ter stick together!"

"Truth be told, darlin', I never wanted to leave England.

SUZANNE G. ROGERS

Don't worry about me. I'll go back ter the East End and make my way somehow. Maybe I really will take ter the stage. Ye can write ter me when ye get settled in America…if ye ever learn to write."

With a wink and a nod, George reached out his hand to his sister. Crying, Betsy grasped his hand as if she would never let it go.

BLEAK HOUSE

*S*everal hatboxes lay open on Jillian's bed, revealing merry bits of colored straw, feathers, and ribbons fashioned into concoctions designed to catch a gentleman's eye. Jillian sat at her dressing table with one such creation on her hair. She cocked her head to one side as she gazed into the mirror, trying to decide which was the most fetching angle to wear her new three-cornered Marquis hat.

Aunt Letty's maid tapped on her door. "Excuse me, miss. A Sir James has come to call."

"Thank you, Alice." Jillian handed her the Marquis hat. "Could you put this away for me?"

As she descended the stairs to the drawing room, Jillian sought to remember where she'd met Sir James. Fortunately, she recognized him right away as one of the young men she'd met during her ride on Rotten Row.

"Jillian, Sir James informs me that Miss Watkins has already introduced you," Aunt Letty said.

"It's a pleasure to see you again, Miss Roring." He gave her a bow.

Jillian returned his bow with a curtsy. She lowered herself into a chair, and he resumed his seat on the horsehair sofa.

"I was just telling Mrs. Marsh how fortuitous it was I should happen to see you both out shopping earlier today," he said. "My club is on Bond Street."

"Ah, yes, this morning my aunt took me to one of the best milliners in London. We lunched afterward at the Empress ladies club on Dover Street. I had a lovely time."

"I'm so glad."

Sir James spent the next few minutes recommending various merchants and places of interest around town. Exactly fifteen minutes later, he took his leave. Aunt Letty waited to speak until after the front door had closed.

"It seems you've made an impression, Jillian. Sir James never would have called upon me if you were not here. Do you like him?"

"He is amiable." Jillian paused. "Erm...perhaps I should have mentioned before, Sophia and I also met Mr. Logan in the park yesterday."

"What?"

"Don't be concerned, Aunt. He and I both behaved as if it was our first introduction."

"That is not the reason for my surprise. I can't help but wonder why Mr. Logan would travel to town unless he means to pursue you?"

"I'm certain he will not. Sophia has changed her mind and says she will accept him after all."

"I would be shocked if he renews his offer to her."

"She *is* extraordinarily beautiful, Aunt."

"As are you."

"That, perhaps, is in the eye of the beholder. And Sophia informs me my connections are insignificant."

"Her connections are no better than yours...*and* she is a jilt."

"She says Mr. Logan is a rake."

"That *is* his reputation, I'll grant you. But now that I've met him, I am not so certain it is accurate."

"You think not?" A weight lifted from Jillian's shoulders. "I suppose I *should* reserve judgment then."

"That would be wise. You cannot rely on Miss Watkins to be wholly disinterested in her assertions about Mr. Logan. She may rightly view you as competition."

"How silly."

"Tell Sarah to lay out something pretty for you to wear tonight. We are attending a play at Toole's Theatre."

"How marvelous! I look forward to some diverting entertainment."

"It is not the time to relax, my girl. Make no mistake, until you are engaged, you are on constant display."

IN THE LOBBY of the theatre, Aunt Letty made sure to introduce Jillian to her beautifully dressed friends. They, in turn, introduced her to their sons and daughters.

"Be as pleasant to the girls as you are to the young gentlemen," whispered Aunt Letty as they were ushered to their seat. "Some of them have eligible brothers."

Jillian suppressed a smile, but her aunt was perfectly serious. As the farcical comedy unfolded on stage, Aunt Letty tapped on Jillian's arm with her fan.

"Keep a composed expression. You're a fool if you believe all opera glasses in use tonight are trained on the actors."

Although she was startled, Jillian did her best to comply. At the end of the evening, however, her ribs hurt from holding in her mirth. Sophia was not among the theatre patrons, fortunately, but she caught herself scanning the crowds for a certain dark-haired gentleman. *Stop it, Jillian. Mr. Logan will not magically appear everywhere you go.* Nevertheless, she couldn't help but wonder if he and Sophia were at a dinner party or dance somewhere together.

~

Logan walked into Sophia's drawing room, but he did not sit. He'd barely set his hat upon a table when Sophia glided into the room and shut the door.

"Thank you for coming so promptly," she said.

He folded his arms across his chest. "I cannot imagine what we have to discuss."

She quickly closed the distance between them.

"Oh come now, Logan. I was so happy to see you out riding the other day. Weren't you the least bit glad to see me again?"

"I thought you looked quite well."

Sophia pouted. "You're still angry, and I don't blame you." Her slender fingers traveled across his shoulder and down the length of his sleeve. "For the sake of Christian charity, can't we put our differences behind us, and carry on as before?"

He leaned over to pick up his hat.

"Don't speak to me of Christian charity, *Miss Watkins*. My behavior toward you shall remain civil, as always, but I shall not seek to deepen our relationship beyond that."

Her face clouded over. "That's very hard-hearted of you."

"Be that as it may." He bowed. "I bid you good evening."

When he opened the drawing room door abruptly, he discovered Mrs. Watkins listening at the door. She jumped back with a guilty start. If Logan weren't so annoyed with Sophia, he would have laughed out loud.

"Beg pardon, madam," he said.

The night air felt refreshing on Logan's face as he walked away from the Watkinses' townhouse. When he'd received Sophia's note begging him to discuss a matter of critical importance earlier, he could not as a gentleman refuse to respond.

Although he still found her exceedingly beautiful, to rekindle their romance was not only impossible, but also unpalatable. For him, her beauty was as attractive as poison. Sophia's touch was unwelcome, and even the fragrance she used seemed noxious to him. *I am completely over her.*

Not wishing to be alone, Logan headed to White's. With no other engagements, he would spend the rest of his evening surrounding by masculine conversation and pursuits.

I shall celebrate my release from Purgatory with a drink.

∿

"Score round one to Sir James," Nelson said. "I understand he called upon the mysterious Miss Roring today."

The smoke filled room at White's was filled with gentlemen at cards, reading newspapers, or nursing after dinner drinks. Logan, Hawkins, and Lord Yardley were engaged in a lively game of Commerce, but they glanced up when Nelson spoke.

"Sir James, you must share what you discovered," Lord Yardley said.

"And give up my advantage? I think not!" Sir James replied, a smile playing on his lips.

Laughter ensued. Mr. Loach, who'd just settled onto a sofa with a brandy, cleared his throat. "Allow me to enlighten you, Lord Yardley. I just came from Toole's Theatre, where my wife and I met Miss Roring. She is the niece of Mrs. Leticia Marsh, and is staying with her for the Season."

"There goes my advantage," Sir James muttered.

"What was your impression of the young lady, Mr. Loach?" Hawkins asked.

"Miss Roring offered her opinion of the play most decidedly." Loach paused for dramatic effect. "But were I twenty years younger and unmarried, I would welcome her opinions on anything."

More laughter.

"I knew her late mother, Miss Katherine Monroe, many years ago. When she began to keep company with Captain Roring, I was quite disappointed," Loach said. "He was a handsome Norwegian devil who had all the ladies atwitter. I believe he has accumulated a vast fortune importing ice."

"The Ice Captain is Miss Roring's father? How intriguing," Hawkins said.

Lord Yardley frowned. "He's a merchant?"

"That is an uncharitable characterization. Queen Victoria welcomes him to the palace whenever he sails into Regent's Canal, and his daughter was presented at court not more than eight weeks ago," said Loach.

"Her Majesty has grown liberal in her old age," Nelson said.

Logan bristled. "If Miss Roring is fit to be presented at court, she's good enough for any gentleman in England."

A long pause ensued.

"I quite agree," said Lord Yardley. He raised his glass. "Here's to the Ice Princess."

Logan drank the toast before returning to his cards. Although he pretended to be absorbed in the game, the conversation about Miss Roring had been torture. To hear her evaluated and weighed on every level grated upon his nerves.

Perhaps I should pay her a call...just to see how she fares.

AT FIVE O'CLOCK on the dot the next afternoon, Logan arrived at Mrs. Marsh's townhouse astride Tuxano. As he roped his horse's reins to the nearest hitching post, Hawkins rode up on his chestnut stallion. Logan gave his friend a withering glance.

"If you're here to pay Miss Roring a call, why don't you ride around the block a time or two until I've left?"

Hawkins dismounted. "Why don't you?"

"I was here first."

"Only by a nose. Besides, I thought you weren't interested in courting Miss Roring."

"It's a social call, not a proposal."

"That's me as well. I say we pay our social call together."

"Fine."

With Hawkins hard on his heels, Logan mounted the steps to the front door. Hawkins lunged past to ring the bell.

"Why didn't you tell me you were planning to call?" he asked as they waited for the maid to answer the door.

"Why didn't you?" Logan replied.

"It must have slipped my mind."

Lord Yardley emerged from Mrs. Marsh's townhouse just then, surprising Logan and Hawkins both. He gave the two gentlemen a smug smile and a bow before passing down the stairs to the sidewalk.

"Carry on, gents."

Logan and Hawkins watched as His Lordship strolled down the street, walking stick in hand.

"It appears we've been outfoxed," Hawkins murmured.

A young maid appeared in the doorway.

"Excuse me, sirs, but the ladies of the house are not receiving any more visitors today. Mrs. Marsh and her niece are getting ready to go out for the evening. If you'd like to leave your cards, I'll make sure my mistress knows you called."

With little choice, Logan and Hawkins handed over their cards and turned away disappointed.

"Oh, well. Perhaps I'll call on Miss Fairley," Hawkins said as he untied his horse. "She lives not two blocks from here."

"I leave you to it, then," Logan replied. "Good luck."

As he rode home, Logan tried to shake off his feeling of frustration. A dinner party at his cousin Caroline's home was his destination for the evening—and he wasn't looking forward to it. His cousin was constantly trying to pair him with eager young debutantes, to no success. He gave a long sigh. Although the event would most assuredly be tedious, at least the food would be good. Hopefully, he'd navigate his way through the party without encountering any clinging young ladies—or insulting Caroline.

~

JILLIAN DESCENDED the stairs in a tightly fitted dinner gown of midnight blue lace, with an accordion-pleat underskirt that billowed out when she walked. Aunt Letty waited for her in the entryway, clad in an elegant champagne-colored Princess gown.

"You look lovely, Jillian," Aunt Letty said, beaming with pleasure.

"As do you, Aunt."

"Thank you." Aunt Letty waved a pair of cards in the air. "We had two gentlemen callers while we were upstairs dressing for dinner."

Jillian wilted when she read the names. "Oh, no! Why didn't they come in time to save me from Lord Yardley?"

"Now, now. His Lordship's visit was an honor."

"Perhaps, but his title cannot make up for his lack of personality."

"He does not possess a sparkling wit, but since men almost never talk to their wives, it's of little consequence."

Jillian's eyebrows lifted. "Aunt, do you mean to tell me you seldom spoke with Uncle Joseph?"

"We led vastly different lives, I'm afraid. My only regret is that we never had children."

The carriage was waiting out front to ferry Jillian and Aunt Letty the short distance to their destination. After they settled themselves onto the seat, the driver urged the horses forward.

"So where is this dinner party, Aunt?" Jillian asked.

"At the home of Mr. and Mrs. Bleak. Mrs. Bleak and I belong to the same garden club."

"Oh, I remember Mrs. Bleak. We attended a tea at her home when I was last in London, didn't we?"

"Your memory serves you well."

Jillian, suddenly pensive, leaned back against the carriage upholstery. The name Bleak reminded her of Dickens, which in turn brought up Logan's image. The afternoon she'd spent discussing literature with him seemed a distant pleasure. Had she realized the rarity of their conversation, perhaps she would have taken care to enjoy it all the more.

"Aunt Letty, do you suppose it's possible to find a loving husband who wants to converse with his wife?"

"Your mother was successful in that regard. Your father retired from the sea shortly after their marriage to spend time with her."

"Did he?"

"He meant to live the life of a gentleman, but after Katherine passed he resumed command of his ship. I believe he couldn't bear to be in England without her."

"That's sad...and romantic."

"Captain Lars Roring never looked at another girl after meeting your mother, although many young ladies plotted and schemed to separate them. He was the toast of London."

"And yet Sophia told me his profession is considered 'trade.'"

Aunt Letty bristled. "She did, did she? He's the captain of a ship, not the man who drives the ice cart." She paused. "I probably shouldn't mention this, but one of the girls who was madly in love with your father was Isabella Hunter. She went on to become Mrs. Watkins."

"Sophia's mother?"

"The very same."

Peals of mirth bubbled up from Jillian's lips, until tears

formed at the corners of her eyes. "Well, that explains a great deal."

~

AS THEY GATHERED in the drawing room before dinner, Caroline introduced Logan to her other guests. One member of the party was a Miss Kelsey, whom he assumed he was to escort in to dinner. The poor girl was horribly shy and practically fainted upon their introduction. As he turned away, he shot his cousin a reproving glance.

"What are you thinking, Caroline?" he said underneath his breath.

"Trust me, Mackenzie," she murmured.

Moments later, a pair of latecomers arrived. Logan felt his feet riveted to the carpet when he recognized Mrs. Marsh and Miss Roring. After another quick round of introductions, Caroline paired her guests for the promenade to the dining room.

"Cousin, will you escort Miss Roring down to dinner?" Caroline asked, a twinkle in her eye.

"Gladly."

As Logan and Jillian descended the stairs to the entry-level floor, he cast about for a topic of conversation.

"This is a fortunate coincidence."

"I'm sorry my aunt and I were unable to receive you and Mr. Hawkins earlier," she said.

"And yet here we are."

"Indeed. I understand my aunt and your cousin belong to the same garden club."

"Ah, well, that explains it. I believe you've met Sir James and Lord Yardley. Mr. Hawkins and I belong to their same gentleman's club."

"It must be a very amiable club to count the four of you amongst its members."

"You're too kind."

The conversation with Miss Roring was innocuous enough, but Logan felt an undercurrent between them. Was it the secret he shared with her that lent an intimacy to their words, or could it be something more?

Could I be falling in love with the girl? Impossible!

THE PARTY at Lord Wisthorne's magnificent home was in full swing. Although the ballroom was filled with dancers, Sophia wove her way through the crowded periphery, trying to avoid the attentions of Vicar Lewis. The earnest vicar was a respectable sort of fellow, but Sophia had no intention of becoming the wife of a clergyman. Nevertheless, her mother insisted she be courteous to him—which he'd mistaken for encouragement. As he drew closer, she ducked behind some concealing window seat drapery. Through the curtain opening, she spied the vicar walk past with a bewildered expression on his face. Unfortunately, two gentlemen paused nearby to chat and she couldn't emerge from her hiding place without being seen. Pouting with frustration, she waited for them to leave... until their conversation became too interesting to ignore.

"So how goes the wager involving Miss Roring?"

"It's too soon to tell, I'm afraid, but I'm still betting on Logan. He will melt the Ice Princess, mark my word."

"I don't know...Lord Yardley and Sir James have entered the fray."

"But no woman can resist Logan when he's on the prowl, title or not."

"No woman except for Miss Watkins."

The men burst into laughter and moved off. Sophia stepped out from behind the drapery, smiling with glee.

BREAKFAST OF DECEIT

*A*s she exchanged small talk with Logan during the dinner party, Jillian continually had to remind herself to concentrate. His very presence had set her senses in a whirl. Her worst fear was she might lose control of her tongue and start babbling nonsense. The temperature of the Julienne soup was nothing compared to the warmth of her cheeks, nor the heat at her core. Although she sipped cool water from her crystal goblet, it did little to abate her emotional upheaval. *I must marshal my feelings lest I embarrass myself! Mr. Logan is all politeness, and he has given you his friendship, nothing more.*

After dinner, the ladies left the gentlemen to their port and cigars and went into the parlor. The separation from Logan was a welcome respite for Jillian, who managed to regain her composure. As Miss Kelsey pounded out a halting version of "Dance of the Sugar Plum Fairy" on the piano, Jillian maneuvered Aunt Letty to one side.

"Did you know Mr. Logan and Mrs. Bleak were cousins?"

"Caroline may have mentioned it."

The tone of Aunt Letty's reply seemed a tad too innocent. Jillian's eyes narrowed.

"Did you suggest to Mrs. Bleak the both of us should be invited here tonight?"

"I don't know what on Earth you're talking about."

Jillian gave her a sidelong glance. "Do you not?"

"No, but it gives you the chance to get to know one another in a different setting," Aunt Letty said. "Caroline told me privately she's never seen her cousin so transfixed as he was when you arrived."

"I'd like to believe her, but I'm afraid he is merely being kind."

"Jillian, I could tell there was some feeling between you and Mr. Logan at Idunn Court. His presence in town confirms it. Give him some encouragement, dear girl. You may have found your match."

A ray of hope broke through the doubts clouding Jillian's brow, and she suddenly felt quite buoyant. Mrs. Bleak asked her to play the piano just as the men began to filter into the parlor. Logan came over to listen, a rapt expression on his face.

"That was simply marvelous," he said after she finished.

"It sounds best with a full orchestra, but 'Morning Mood' by Norwegian composer Edvard Grieg is one of my favorite pieces. It depicts a sunrise," Jillian said.

"Yes, I could hear that as you played. Well done."

Jillian rose from the piano to allow Mrs. Bleak to be seated next. As the party grew noisier, Logan was obliged to lean in toward Jillian to be heard. His breath as he spoke tickled her cheek and ear. A delicious shiver traveled down her spine.

"Will you walk with me a bit, Miss Roring? My cousin keeps a beautiful courtyard out back. There is a view of it from the balcony."

Jillian's stomach gave a little lift. Her assent was on her lips, but her eyes flicked a glance at Aunt Letty. An almost imperceptible nod from her aunt gave her permission to accompany Logan for a stroll.

"Mr. Logan, I believe I would enjoy some fresh air."

~

STRAINS OF MOZART accompanied them as Logan escorted Jillian down the hall. Her subtle fragrance filled his senses; was it honeysuckle or perhaps jasmine?

"Your cousin plays well," Jillian said.

"I believe it's the only song Caroline knows. At least it's the only one I've ever heard her play since we were children." He gave Jillian a wink.

Jillian laughed. "You're teasing."

"A little."

As they stepped out onto the balcony, the flickering gaslight from the townhouse illuminated the small topiary and flowerbeds lining the small courtyard below.

"Aunt Letty says gaslight makes ladies more attractive," Jillian said.

"I don't know about that, but I've never seen you look more beautiful."

"Thank you. It's a far cry from my mud-smeared traveling suit, isn't it?"

"The mud was rather endearing, actually." A long silence ensued. "Are you..." He paused for a moment before clearing his throat. "Have you definitely made up your mind against me, Miss Roring?"

Her eyes grew wide. "What do you mean?"

Logan took her hand. At the touch of her bare skin, his heart began to pound.

"You rejected my proposal before because you believed me to be indifferent. Will you give me the opportunity to convince you otherwise?"

Her blue eyes seemed to look straight into his soul. "I can think of nothing that would give me more pleasure."

His fingertips worshipped the contour of her cheek and traced a path to her mouth.

"I could scarcely taste my food tonight, thinking about kissing these lips," he murmured.

"I could scarcely draw breath, wishing that you would."

His head bent toward hers, but before their lips met a voice rang out from down the hall.

"Jillian, we need you for cards."

Disappointment was written on Jillian's features. "Yes, Aunt Letty. I shall be in directly."

Logan kissed Jillian with undisguised passion. *I defy her to label me indifferent now!* It took all his strength to step back. "You'd better go in."

Jillian swayed toward him a moment before following her aunt's footsteps. Logan breathed in the cool nighttime air as he stared at the moon.

I love her.

JILLIAN FLOATED DOWN THE HALLWAY, fairly bursting with happiness. *Mr. Logan means to court me, without any sense of obligation or pity this time.* Her lips tingled deliciously from her first kiss. Her behavior would not be considered proper, of course, but Jillian could not bring herself to regret letting Logan take the liberty. *In fact, I hope he does it again as soon as possible!*

As she was seated at the card table, she wondered if anyone else could perceive the happiness she felt inside. Out of the corner of her eye, she saw Logan enter the parlor. She forced her attention onto her cards, lest anyone notice her blush. Would he pay her a call tomorrow afternoon? Jillian mentally went through her wardrobe, trying to decide which frock he would like best. She hadn't yet worn the low-cut afternoon dress the same color as her eyes. Its neckline made the most of

her long, slender neck and décolleté. She smiled with antic-
ipation.

I can hardly wait.

~

AUNT LETTY and Jillian arose early the next morning to attend a
ladies' breakfast. Alice helped Jillian dress in a modest dove gray
and white blouse with a matching gray skirt. As the maid
brushed out her hair, Jillian examined her reflection in the
mirror. Slight smudges underneath her eyes revealed her lack of
sleep, but she didn't mind in the least. All night long a sense of
giddiness had consumed her. It was as if she'd bathed in champagne and her skin was still tingling from the bubbles.

Is this what being in love is like? If so, I want more.

Jillian hurried downstairs, where her aunt was waiting in the
parlor.

"Good morning, Aunt Letty!" Jillian's smile was broad.

"Good morning, Jillian. The carriage is being brought
around just now." Aunt Letty peered at her. "You certainly are in
a good mood today."

"I had a wonderful time at Mrs. Bleak's dinner party."

"I suspect Mr. Logan can take credit for your ebullience."

"Oh, Aunt, he means to woo me!"

"After that kiss, I should hope so."

Jillian felt her face burning. "You saw?"

"No, but I suspected as much. Congratulations, my dear. It's
not every girl who gets engaged in her first Season."

"Let us not get ahead of ourselves, Aunt!"

As Aunt Letty's carriage set off, Jillian smiled at anyone
passing by, including street venders and policemen. Her aunt
pretended not to notice. After a short journey, their carriage
joined the queue at Lady Wimpel's home on the outskirts of
Mayfair.

"My heavens, I didn't realize there would be so many guests," Jillian said.

"Lady Wimpel knows everybody who's anybody. She rang me up personally to make sure you and I would be attending. It seems she's eager to meet the young lady who has taken London by storm."

"I can't think who she means."

Aunt Letty chuckled. "Your modesty does you credit." She paused. "Your mother was considered a great beauty as well. I was proud to be her elder sister, and I'm proud to be your aunt."

Jillian squeezed her hand. "And I'm lucky to be your niece."

Although she tried not to gape when she was admitted to Lady Wimpel's home, Jillian found it difficult. The magnificent home was of classic Grecian design, complete with polished marble and tasteful artwork, and the guests had turned out in their best attire. When she spied a young matron wearing glittering jewels, Jillian suddenly wondered if her own attire wasn't too plain.

Aunt Letty followed her gaze. "Oh, dear," she whispered. "It's too early for diamonds, but Mrs. Stillwood is new money and always tries overly hard."

Lady Wimpel was at the entrance of the ballroom, greeting her guests as they entered. When Aunt Letty introduced her to Jillian, the woman gave her a warm smile.

"Now I understand what has the gentlemen all in uproar," she said. "The loveliest hothouse orchid cannot compare to you, Miss Roring."

At such effusive praise, Jillian felt the blood rush to her cheeks.

"I thank you, Lady Wimpel. It's an honor to make your acquaintance."

"Such pretty manners. You and your aunt are seated at my table, my dear."

A servant escorted Jillian and Aunt Letty to the round table for twelve at one end of the hall. To Jillian's dismay, Sophia and her mother were already seated there. Was it her imagination, or did Sophia and Mrs. Watkins exchange a sly glance as she approached?

"Good morning," Sophia sang out. "Come sit next to me, Jillian. I want to hear all your news, and then I shall tell you mine."

Privately, Jillian had no interest in exchanging confidences with Sophia, but she smiled nevertheless. The breakfast was more like a banquet, with all manner of elaborately prepared dishes. Baskets of breads and muffins had been set out on the table, along with butter and marmalade. Servants appeared at Jillian's elbow at frequent intervals with delightful offerings such as bacon, pheasant pie, sausage, ham, kippers, haddock in puff pastry, deviled kidneys, and eggs cooked several different ways. Jillian's delicate china cup was continuously replenished with tea, although Aunt Letty took coffee instead. Sophia drank hot chocolate, and the fragrance kept wafting in Jillian's direction.

Lady Wimpel entertained the table with stories about her recent sojourn to Paris. Jillian hadn't exchanged more than a few words with Sophia during the entire meal, and began to think she would be able to forego the pleasure entirely. When she excused herself to go freshen up, unfortunately Sophia decided to accompany her.

"I adore your dress," Sophia said as they left the ballroom. "Its plainness draws attention to your face."

Jillian bit her tongue at the backhanded compliment. "Thank you, Sophia. Tell me, have you been riding of late?"

"No, but I went to a ball last night."

"I'm certain it was great fun."

"Yes, but I did hear a bit of information I thought you should know."

Without warning, Sophia grabbed Jillian's wrist, pulled her

into the nearby library, and shut the door. "Has Mr. Logan called on you?"

"Er...why do you ask?"

"At the ball last night, I overheard an interesting conversation. It seems you are the focus of a wager amongst the gentlemen."

"What?"

"Apparently Mr. Logan is considered the favorite to win your affections. I know from personal experience just how competitive he can be."

If Sophia had thrown a glass of cold water in Jillian's face, she couldn't have been more shocked.

"I-I simply cannot believe it, Sophia. You must have heard it wrong."

"Sir James and Lord Yardley are part of the wager, too. Have you by chance received a call from them?"

Jillian glanced away.

"Ha! I knew it. And that's not all...they've nicknamed you Ice Princess." Sophia giggled. "I'm not entirely certain it was a compliment."

Moisture began to sting Jillian's eyes. "You've said enough, Sophia."

"I'm terribly sorry, but it's best you learn of Mr. Logan's deceit from a friend before he has the opportunity to take advantage of you." She paused. "If it's any consolation, Mr. Logan won the wager last year too—with his engagement to me."

Jillian turned away from Sophia just as a teardrop rolled down her cheek. She wiped it away surreptitiously with trembling fingers.

"Thank you for telling me. I'd like to be alone for a moment, if you don't mind."

"Oh, dear, you're upset. I'm only trying to spare you my fate, Jillian."

Sophia opened the library door and disappeared. Jillian sank into a chair. Her emotions waved from disbelief to fury and back again, much like a game of lawn tennis. *Sophia is inventing a falsehood! Since she wishes to secure Mr. Logan for herself, she has every reason to separate me from him. Her assertions cannot be believed. On the other hand, how could Sophia know Lord Yardley and Sir James had come to call unless she'd heard it from someone in their inner circle? No...it must be true! So they mock me with the name of Ice Princess, do they? Was it Mr. Logan who dreamed up the endearment? He has been discussing me with his friends, using our prior acquaintance to gain a hidden advantage in a game of sport. I clearly did not conceal how I felt about him well enough and he played upon those feelings last night. How utterly despicable of him! I'm such a stupid fool, and I've characterized Sophia unfairly.*

By the time Jillian returned to the ballroom, the breakfast banquet had concluded and half the guests had already departed. Aunt Letty rushed over, a worried look on her face.

"Are you all right, dear? When Miss Watkins returned to the table without you, I became concerned."

"Yes, Aunt. I just have a headache. Let us say our good-byes. I'd like to go home."

LOGAN BOLTED from his bed with a surge of energy. His feeling of elation made it difficult to eat breakfast. Instead, he went riding in Hyde Park, letting Tuxano gallop to his heart's content. He would have liked nothing better than to pay a call to Miss Roring afterward, but propriety dictated he wait until late afternoon. As the morning passed, Logan debated the best way to woo Miss Roring. Should he ask her to accompany him to a large, public event such as the opera or the symphony? Or would it be better to begin in a more intimate setting, such as an author reading, lunch at a café, or an art show at a small gallery?

So many possibilities tumbled through his mind, he could not arrive at a conclusion. He finally elected to suggest a few outings and let Miss Roring decide according to her taste.

When he contemplated the quirk of fate that had brought her into his life, he could not believe his good fortune. Considering his despair a few short weeks ago, the contrast was marked and profound. Had she traveled with him to London, Mrs. Lyman would have laughed to see him so chipper and cheerful. *I could spend a lifetime admiring Miss Roring and it would not be enough time to show her how completely she has captured my heart.* When he compared his current feelings with those he'd had for Sophia, he was ashamed. He'd been so caught up in the chase last Season, he'd not perceived Sophia's fickle and deceitful nature. Back then, he'd cursed fate at the ruins of his engagement, unaware that he'd been taken into fate's benevolent bosom.

He jotted off a note of thanks for the dinner party to his cousin Caroline. He sent one of his servants to deliver it, along with a robust bouquet of dark pink roses to convey his gratitude. Although he didn't mention Miss Roring in the letter, he wished he could compliment Caroline on what role she herself had played in his current happiness. The memory of the kiss he'd exchanged with Miss Roring was still fresh on his lips. He felt so magnanimous, after he'd donned a fresh suit in which to call on Miss Roring, Logan gave Ian the rest of the night off.

Along the way to Eaton Square, Logan stopped his hired cab at the flower stand on the corner. He agonized between choosing purple lilacs to reveal his first emotions of love or light pink roses, to convey his passion. He finally selected the lilacs, so as not to seem presumptuous. The fresh lilacs were nothing to Miss Roring's perfection, of course, but perhaps she would welcome a token of his esteem. As the hansom cab pulled up in front of Mrs. Marsh's townhouse, Logan asked the driver to wait. He bounded up the steps, rang the doorbell, and straightened his cravat. A few moments later, the housekeeper opened the door, took his card, and showed him into the drawing room. Unable to relax, Logan paced a bit. He felt rather foolish with the lilacs still clutched in his hand, but he wanted to give them to Miss Roring personally.

Jillian's aunt entered the drawing room with an expression so somber Logan's smile faded instantly.

"Mrs. Marsh, are you unwell?"

"Perfectly so, Mr. Logan. I regret to inform you that neither Miss Roring nor I will be receiving you today or any time in the future. Have I made myself clear?"

LORD ARCHIE

A clammy chill spread from the top of Logan's head to the soles of his feet.

"I'm sorry, but I don't understand you. What has happened?"

Jillian appeared in the doorway just then. Her color was extremely pale and her eyes red and slightly swollen, as if from weeping. Panic seized Logan's heart.

"Miss Roring, what is wrong?"

"Aunt Letty, will you leave us for a few moments?"

"Are you sure?"

At Jillian's nod, Aunt Letty gave Logan one last, withering look and left.

"For Heaven's sake, Miss Roring, tell me what is troubling you!" Logan exclaimed.

He tried to keep the pleading note from his voice, but he was unsuccessful. He laid the lilacs on the mantle and crossed to Jillian, but she held up her hands to keep him at bay.

"I have been informed that a wager has been placed on who will be the first to win my favor. For you to treat my feelings in such a shabby manner is cruel. I will not be treated like a racehorse, Mr. Logan, and I beg you not to have any further contact with me."

Logan stared at her, aghast. "Who told you this?"

"That is unimportant. Do you deny it?"

"Yes, I deny it insofar as my involvement! There was some good-natured discussion of a wager, but I refused to be part of it, I assure you. You may ask Mr. Hawkins for confirmation."

"I would expect him to take your part in this, since he is your friend."

"He is a gentleman and would not lie for me or anyone else!"

"Just like you didn't lie to me about the truth of your broken engagement to Miss Watkins?"

"She told you?"

Jillian's chin lifted. "I also discovered my nickname amongst your acquaintances is Ice Princess."

Logan was astonished. "It was meant as the highest compliment, I assure you."

"I'm sorry to snatch your erstwhile victory away, Mr. Logan. I'm sure my conquest would have added greatly to your reputation as a rake."

Logan picked up his hat.

"I can see there is no convincing you of my innocence in this business. You paint me unfairly, Miss Roring. Before I leave, let me say that my intentions toward you have always been sincere and wholesome."

But Jillian merely whirled around and fled the drawing room, leaving Logan to find his way out. Numb, he stumbled down the stairs to the sidewalk, narrowly avoiding disaster by gripping the handrail. The driver jumped from the cab.

"Are you all right, Guv'nor?"

Logan nodded and allowed the man to guide him into the cab.

"Take me to White's."

"Straightaway."

The idea of drinking in the company of whoever had betrayed him suddenly seemed unappealing.

"On second thought, take me to Boodle's."

JILLIAN TOOK her place at the table when she was called to dinner, but the food on her plate remained untouched. Aunt Letty gave her niece a sympathetic glance.

"You must eat a little. You'll need your strength at the ball tonight."

"I will be horrible company. Can I not beg off?"

"You do not want to give offense, my dear. It's the Duke and Duchess of Rochester."

"I'm a mess, Aunt. My skin is blotchy, and my eyes are red. How am I ever to appear presentable?"

"You'll have a nice hot bath. Afterward, a little powder, a bit of rouge, and some lip pomade will perk up your looks. A burnt matchstick will darken your lashes, too."

"Aunt Letty!"

Her aunt gave her a mischievous look. "There is not a lady worth her salt who does not resort to a little help now and again. Besides, Jillian, you cannot give the gossips free rein. If knowledge of that silly wager is widespread, your disheartened demeanor will confirm Mr. Logan broke your heart. Is that what you want?"

"No."

When Jillian's eyes began to swim with tears again, Aunt Letty patted her hand.

"That's enough of that. If Her Majesty can bear up under the grief of losing her husband, you can forge through your current distress."

"But in fact the queen does not bear her loss well. She's been in mourning these past thirty-eight years."

"Oh well, you understand my meaning. Now eat something and I'll have Alice bring you a glass of champagne while you're in the bath."

∽

MOROSE, Logan sat in front of one of the fireplaces in Boodle's and nursed his gin. The day had begun in a spectacular fashion and had ended in disaster. Miss Roring could not have intimate knowledge of what had transpired in White's unless someone who'd been there had told her. Only the culprit had twisted the words so they'd taken on a sinister overtone. One of his friends had betrayed him, but why? The biggest mystery, however, was how Miss Roring had known his broken engagement was a deception. The only people who knew the actual events were himself, Sophia…and her lover. As a gentleman, Logan had allowed Sophia to announce publicly she'd jilted him. Most certainly she would not have freely confessed otherwise to anyone, since to do so would mean her absolute downfall.

He'd parted from Miss Roring after midnight last night, so she had to get her information sometime prior to his arrival at five o'clock today. If only he knew what schedule she'd kept before then, perhaps he could discover who had been feeding Miss Roring lies. Neither Mrs. Marsh nor Miss Roring were likely to tell him, but a member of the household staff might be persuaded if the price was high enough. Logan wracked his brain as he tried to remember the name of the maid Miss Roring had mentioned during dinner. Was it Elspeth, or perhaps Eliza? No—it was Alice! If he could speak with her privately, Alice would be able to tell him what he needed to know.

His timepiece indicated it was after eight. Mrs. Marsh and Miss Roring would have left the townhouse for the evening if they'd made plans. Surely since her aunt was so keen to marry her off, she would make certain her niece was out tonight some-where conspicuous. Intent on his investigation, Logan abandoned the remainder of his gin, departed Boodle's, and made his way to Eaton Square.

As Jillian rode in the carriage with Aunt Letty, she tried unsuccessfully to tug up the neckline of her gown.

"Leave it alone, girl!" Aunt Letty exclaimed.

"I feel so naked. Everybody will be staring at my décolleté."

"That's the whole point. Would you come all this way just to hide under a table?"

"If I didn't know better, Aunt, I might suspect you were quite wild in your youth."

"How do you suppose I landed Mr. Marsh? Your mother got the looks in our family, so I had only my décolleté and determination to work with."

The effects of the champagne made Jillian giggle. Her mirth was infectious and finally Aunt Letty laughed too.

"I'm glad you've cheered up."

"I'm not cheerful in the least," Jillian said. "It's just that my head is spinning."

"Good enough. Make sure to drink water or plain punch from now on. Silliness is fine, but public intoxication in a young lady is unattractive in the extreme."

Mrs. Marsh's housekeeper gave Logan a cool stare. "The ladies of the house are not at home, sir."

"That's all right. I'm actually here to speak with Alice, if I may."

"It's late, and the help are not allowed gentlemen callers."

The door started to close, but Logan stuck his foot in the opening.

"I just want to see her a moment, right here on the doorstep if necessary." He produced a ten-pound note and pressed it into the servant's hand. "That's for your trouble."

The housekeeper gaped at the money, which represented the lion's share of her annual salary. The woman slid it into her apron pocket.

"Wait here, sir."

The door shut and Logan paced. At length, the door opened a crack and a wide-eyed Alice peeked out.

"Can I help you, sir?"

Her voice was timid. Logan reassured her by producing another ten-pound note. The girl nearly choked when she saw the money.

"Take that to the East End if you're looking for easy company, sir!" she exclaimed.

"No, Alice. All I want is information." He laid a five-pound note on top of the ten. "Can you tell me what Miss Roring's schedule was today?"

A light of recognition shone in her eyes. "I know you... you're that Mr. Logan. You've treated the young mistress ill, if you'll pardon my saying so!"

"It's all been a horrible misunderstanding, Alice, and I'm trying to get to the bottom of it. What of her schedule?"

Alice chewed her lip.

"Well the morning started out well enough. Mrs. Marsh and Miss Roring went to a ladies' breakfast. When they came back, Miss Roring was in a great deal of distress...and blackened your name something terrible."

"Can you tell me whose breakfast she attended?"

"Erm, that would be Lady Wimpel, I believe. Mrs. Marsh says she knows everybody who's anybody."

"Yes, I am well acquainted with Lady Wimpel."

Logan fell silent as he absorbed Alice's response. Sophia would most certainly have been in attendance at any function of Lady Wimpel's. That would explain how Jillian knew about his engagement, but it didn't account for the rest. Perhaps manipulative Sophia had extracted the information out of one of his gormless friends and twisted it to suit her purposes.

"It all fits," he murmured.

"Is there anything else, Mr. Logan?" Alice asked.

"Where is Miss Roring right now?"

"She is at a ball this evening, given by the Duke and Duchess of Rochester."

Logan winced. "Is that tonight? With everything going on, I'd forgotten about it. Thank you, Alice. You've been very helpful."

He darted down the stairs.

"I hope it works out for you, sir," Alice called out before shutting the door.

THE ROCHESTER MANSION reminded Jillian of a magnificent palace, with its high ceilings, sweeping staircases, oversized oil paintings, and crystal chandeliers. Music, furnished by a full orchestra, spilled out from the ballroom. Glittering, beautifully dressed people were gathering inside the ballroom. Others were across the hall, chatting in an almost equally large room set up with banquet tables and all manner of food. Jillian giggled when she saw the decorative ice sculptures, since they were almost certainly carved from ice imported by her father.

Aunt Letty had introduced her to the Duke and Duchess of Rochester in the receiving line, as well as their eldest son, Lord Archibald. The young man shocked Jillian when he took her gloved hand, bowed slightly, and brought her fingers to his lips. His burnished gold hair gave him an almost angelic glow, but the fire in his blue eyes conjured a more wicked nature. Instead of pulling her hand away at the familiarity, Jillian found herself smiling in response. *Not Gypsy eyes, but magnetic all the same.* Since there were many more people waiting in the receiving line, there was no opportunity for further conversation, but she hoped Lord Archibald might seek her out for a dance or two at some point during the evening.

As Jillian moved on, she caught sight of her reflection in a tall mirror. Alice and Aunt Letty had worked very hard to make her stunning. Her off the shoulder gown was the palest shell pink, with a tight, shaped bodice. Layers of pink and white netting cascaded to the floor. Dainty crystals sewn to the fabric glinted in the light as she turned, giving the gown a shimmering appearance. Her curled hair was caught up into jeweled combs and arranged into an artful display in the back. Her darkened lashes set off her eyes, and a very light dusting of powder and judicious application of rouge had eased the ravages from her emotional outburst. A simple choker necklace fashioned of fuchsia ribbon was fastened around her throat, and an impressive diamond bracelet gleamed at her wrist.

"I confess I feel quite splendid, Aunt," she said. "Thank you for loaning me your jewelry."

"You're quite welcome. It suits you perfectly."

A gentleman passing by bore a resemblance to Logan, and Jillian felt a sudden pang of longing.

"Aunt Letty, might I have just a little more champagne?"

"Absolutely not. You've had too much as it is."

Sophia's voice rang out just then. "Jillian!" She hastened over, a vision in a gown of claret. "Good evening, Mrs. Marsh."

Aunt Letty inclined her head. "Miss Watkins. If you'll excuse me, young ladies, I see a friend of mine has just arrived."

As Aunt Letty headed off, Sophia extended her gloved hand to squeeze Jillian's.

"I wasn't sure if I would see you tonight, but here you are. Your gown is astonishing! Is it a Charles Worth original?"

"I believe so."

"Mine, too." She scanned the crowd, warily. "I must ask you to keep an eye out for Vicar Lewis. He takes every opportunity to monopolize me."

"Poor Vicar Lewis. I suppose he cannot take a hint."

"Or will not! I heard a rumor that Lord Archibald kissed your hand, is it true?"

"Why, yes."

Sophia frowned, almost imperceptibly. "I suppose when you're royalty, you can get away with things like that."

"Are you acquainted with Lord Archibald?" Jillian asked.

"To some respects. Tell me, has anyone signed your dance card yet?"

"No, I just arrived." Jillian consulted the little fan-shaped booklet dangling from her wrist. "Oh, good, there are plenty of waltzes. I do so love to waltz."

Lord Archibald appeared at her elbow.

"I couldn't help but overhear. I shall instruct the orchestra to play waltzes all night long if you'll dance each and every one of them with me, Miss Roring," he said.

A peculiar expression descended over Sophia's face. "Please excuse me. I must go sample the punch." She threaded her way through the crowd toward the refreshment tables.

Lord Archibald smiled at Jillian and withdrew a pencil from his pocket. "May I?"

She offered him her dance card, and he made several scribbles. A quick glance at the card revealed he had claimed her for the Promenade, two waltzes, a polka, and several quadrilles.

"Forgive me, but it will raise eyebrows if we dance more than three dances together," she said, laughing.

"Blast. It *is* my party, after all," he said. "But if you insist, I will hold you only to the waltzes and the Promenade."

"Thank you for understanding."

~

A TRIO of young ladies standing next to the punch bowl cast curious glances at Lord Archibald and Jillian. As Sophia poured herself a cup of the icy sweet liquid, she overheard their whispers.

"Lord Archibald seems quite taken with that girl. Do either of you know who she is?"

"I heard someone say she's Mrs. Marsh's niece."

"We are not acquainted, but I noticed her at Lady Wimpel's breakfast this morning. She is striking, to say the least, and I adore her gown."

Sophia joined the group.

"Hello, Miss Taylor, Miss Dooney, and Miss Byron." She curtsied. "I heard you mention the lady speaking with Lord Archibald right now."

"Do you know her, Miss Watkins?"

"Very little. Miss Roring is pretty, I grant you. Unfortunately, her father is a common merchant."

The three girls drew back in horror.

"No! Really?"

"I'm afraid so. He's a foreigner who trades in ice and I'm not even certain he speaks English," Sophia said.

"How vulgar!"

"Gentlemen who know Miss Roring call her the Ice Princess in secret...but please don't repeat that to anyone."

"Your confidence is safe with us."

"In my opinion, Lord Archibald is wasting his time with her," Sophia said. "The Duke and Duchess would never consent to such a lowly match." She drained her cup and set it down on a nearby tray. "Enjoy the party, ladies."

Sophia strolled off, secure in the knowledge that the girls with whom she spoke were three of the biggest gossips in London.

HEADWINDS

*L*ord Archibald escorted Jillian into the ballroom, where the dancing was about to commence. She marveled at the domed fresco-painted ceiling, the sparkling chandeliers, the polished wooden floor, and the arched windows lining one side of the room. Tall, lit candelabras accented the arched alcoves on the other side of the ballroom, in which chairs had been arranged. The colorful gowns and jewelry worn by matrons and young ladies alike dazzled the eye.

"You are glowing from within, Miss Roring," Lord Archibald said. "Dare I hope your happiness is due to my presence?"

"I would not have you think otherwise, sir, but I believe no small part of my delight stems from the fact that this is my first ball in London."

"Hurrah for firsts, then."

Jillian studied her escort's profile a moment. *Lord Archibald is perhaps not so magnetically attractive to me as a certain country gentleman, but he is attentive, handsome, and charming. Is it possible I've grown tired of Mr. Logan's brooding good looks?*

As the couples lined up, Jillian noticed Sophia was paired

with the Duke of Rochester. Jillian smiled, but Sophia failed to acknowledge her. Although Jillian was taken back at the slight, she tried to shrug it off. *Sophia was rather cool when Lord Archibald came to speak with me. Could her pique have anything to do with him?*

The music commenced, and Jillian forgot everything else but the Grand Promenade. The dance, designed specifically for ladies to display their charms, was not especially intricate. Many admiring glances were cast Jillian's way, and she silently thanked Aunt Letty for her selection of gown. Halfway through the promenade, she spotted a gentleman resembling Logan amongst the onlookers. Her heart nearly stopped until she gave herself a shake. *Silly girl. You mustn't drop into a dead faint every time you see a head of dark wavy hair!* As the dance brought her closer, her stomach seemed to lift into her throat. Logan had indeed arrived at the ball, his eyes piercing through whatever defenses she'd marshaled against him. Her heart beat faster, and she tore her gaze away. *How am I to get through the entire evening with him here?*

When the opening dance ended, Jillian sank into a curtsy. Lord Archibald bowed and extended his arm.

"If you insist, I shall relinquish you to your aunt for now," he said. "Do you know where she is sitting?"

"I believe she sits in the alcove nearest to the door."

Lord Archibald led Jillian through the crowd. As they approached Aunt Letty, Jillian froze. Logan had positioned himself in the chair next to Aunt Letty, and they were deep in conversation.

"Is there something wrong?" Lord Archibald asked.

Jillian desperately scanned the faces nearby, looking for an acquaintance. Relief flowed through her when she saw a forlorn Miss Kelsey standing alone.

"No, it's just that must speak to a friend of mine. If you'll excuse me, Lord Archibald."

"Do call me Archie." He kissed her hand again. "Thank you for the dance."

Jillian made a beeline for Miss Kelsey and linked her arm through hers.

"Miss Kelsey, you look lovely. Would you be so kind as to accompany me to the ladies' sitting room? I need a moment to freshen up."

Before she could leave the ballroom, three gentlemen of Jillian's acquaintance stopped her to reserve a dance. Because she was with Miss Kelsey, the gentlemen felt obliged to reserve a dance with her as well. Although she was aware the requests were out of courtesy, with each fresh name written on her dance card, Miss Kelsey's eyes grew brighter. As they left the ballroom, she squeezed Jillian's hand.

"I do believe I wouldn't be dancing at all this evening if not for you, Miss Roring," she murmured. "I'm very grateful."

Jillian giggled. "I'm not certain you realize how pretty you are. After you are seen on the dance floor, I expect you will not sit down the rest of the night."

A LARGE MUSIC room had been pressed into service as a ladies' sitting room for the duration of the ball. The walls were already paneled with mirrors, and dressing screens were arranged to afford some measure of privacy. Jillian found an unoccupied area and pretended to preen while she collected herself. Miss Kelsey perched on a nearby settee. Gossip flowed as young ladies chatted a louder than decorum would dictate.

"Lord Archibald is absolutely fawning over that girl. I heard her father is in *trade*."

Jillian blanched.

"To me she looks like a porcelain doll."

"They call her Ice Princess behind her back, I'm told."

At that, laughter ensued.

"That's too cruel, but it fits!"

The voices faded as the girls returned to the ballroom. A comforting arm suddenly slid around Jillian's waist.

"Let's sit for a while, Miss Roring," Miss Kelsey murmured in a soothing tone. "Neither of us is engaged for the second dance."

"Yes, I…"

Shaking from head to toe, Jillian allowed Miss Kelsey to lead her to the settee.

"Would you like me to fetch Mrs. Marsh?"

The vision of Logan in a tête-à-tête with Aunt Letty flashed into Jillian's mind. "No, I don't want to burden her. She warned me that society gossips could be uncharitable."

"Don't listen to those jealous harpies. You're beautiful, talented, sweet, and kind."

"Thank you." Jillian smiled. "May I call you by your Christian name?"

"It's Katherine. Katie, if you like."

"My name is Jillian."

"Ooh, even your name is pretty."

Jillian's smile broadened. "If you hadn't been here, Katie, I might have burst into tears just now."

"I'll wait with you as long as you like."

A glance in the mirror revealed a stain of color on Jillian's cheeks that had nothing to do with the rouge she wore. Although she would have liked nothing better than to flee, she rose and squared her shoulders.

"No, let's go back. I'm not a sea captain's daughter for nothing, you know. I shall stiffen my resolve and sail in the headwinds bravely."

"That's the spirit!"

Let's hope I do not capsize.

The second dance, a quadrille, was underway by the time Jillian and Katie returned to the ballroom. Aunt Letty had left her seat and was dancing with Mr. Loach. *Why she dances beautifully,* Jillian thought. Logan was nowhere to be seen. Perhaps Aunt Letty had given him a verbal trouncing and he'd had the good manners to depart. A vague sense of disappointment ensued, surprising Jillian with its poignancy. *How can I feel his absence so keenly after he exposed me to ridicule?*

Vicar Lewis was chatting with Sophia nearby, gazing at her with slavish adoration. Although Jillian's first impulse was to laugh at Sophia's pained expression, she took pity on her instead.

"Excuse me, Vicar, but I must beg Miss Watkins' assistance," Jillian said. "Sophia, Miss Smith is waiting for you in the ladies' sitting room. I believe she needs your help with her hair."

"Oh, *thank* you, Jillian." Sophia's gratitude was heartfelt. "I shall go to Miss Smith's aid immediately."

To the vicar's obvious disappointment, Sophia hastened off.

SOPHIA SLIPPED INTO THE LADIES' sitting room and found an unoccupied mirror. She smoothed her hair, straightened her gown, and checked her teeth. She was about to step out from behind the wooden screen when she heard her name mentioned.

"Did you see Miss Roring rescue Miss Watkins from Vicar Lewis just now?"

"I saw the whole thing! If only Miss Roring knew what Miss Watkins is saying about her, she wouldn't be so kind."

"Sophia Watkins ought to be ashamed of herself."

"I don't think she cares. Look at the way she jilted Mr. Logan. Her heart must be a lump of black coal."

Sophia turned back toward the mirror. Although her toilette was immaculate, she frowned.

~

"Look, Jillian, there's Mr. Logan with his friend," Katie whispered. "They are heading this way."

Jillian flinched at Logan's approach. *The very sight of him excites my pulse and dulls my wits. It is not fair he should be so frightfully handsome!*

Logan stopped in front of Katie, with Hawkins close at hand.

"My friend has expressed a wish to be acquainted with you, Miss Kelsey," he said. "Hawkins, allow me to present Miss Kelsey. Miss Kelsey, this is Mr. Hawkins."

With a shy smile, Katie curtsied. "Hello, Mr. Hawkins."

"May I reserve a dance or two, Miss Kelsey?" Hawkins asked.

Blushing furiously, Katie extended her dance card. Hawkins peered at it a moment and scribbled his name on three empty lines.

"I cannot believe my luck. The next two dances are mine, as well as the ending Quadrille."

As Hawkins and Katie made small talk, Logan's green eyes turned to Jillian.

"Good evening, Miss Roring."

"Good evening, sir."

The coolness of her tone would have sent most men scurrying off, but Logan remained steadfast.

"Would you allow me a waltz?"

"I'm afraid that all my waltzes are spoken for."

"The Polka Esmeralda, then?"

"I believe in fact my dance card is completely filled, Mr. Logan."

"Oh, that's not so, Jillian," Katie blurted. "I took a peek at your card and there are still a few spots open."

Although Logan's slight smirk invited Jillian to slap his face, she restrained herself.

"My mistake," she said.

She extended the card, and Logan glanced it over.

"I say, that's abominably rude of Archie to monopolize you." He used his pencil to cross out Lord Archibald's name and write his own instead. "The next dance is a waltz, and I claim it for myself."

"Mr. Logan!"

"Yes, Miss Roring?"

"You cannot be serious."

"I am perfectly so."

The quadrille ended. As Hawkins led Katie onto the dance floor, she cast an apologetic glance back at Jillian. Logan held out his gloved hand. "Shall we, Miss Roring?"

Lord Archibald arrived just then.

"Forgive me, Mackenzie, but the lady has promised this waltz to me."

His expression and tone were cordial, but underneath was an undercurrent of steel. Logan smiled pleasantly.

"Perhaps so, Archie, but you may still content yourself with the six other dances she's promised you. I beg you to yield."

Lord Archibald chuckled, but a muscle in his jaw quivered.

"I shall not yield, and I would remind you to defer to your betters."

"Should I meet one of my betters, I would. Since it's *you*, however, I need not bother."

To the casual onlooker, the two gentlemen were having a jovial conversation, but Jillian heard every word. In a rush to avoid a scene, she took Logan's hand.

"Please, Archie, let us indulge Mr. Logan this once."

Lord Archibald's eyes peered at Logan, glittering with dislike. Nevertheless, he bowed to Jillian. "As you wish, Miss Roring."

Triumphant at last, Logan led Jillian out on the floor.

"Have you lost your mind, sir?" she murmured.

"That's entirely possible."

"Your incivility toward Lord Archibald in his own home is breathtaking. What if he chooses to retaliate against you?"

"He will not. It just so happens I hold a bit of information over his head that would inconvenience him greatly should it ever become publicly known."

Logan's hand slid around her waist.

"I've maneuvered to get you on the dance floor because I knew it was the only way you would listen to me."

The music commenced, and they began to dance together.

"I've deduced it was Miss Watkins who told you of the supposed wager."

Jillian kept her eyes firmly fixed somewhere over Logan's shoulder, unable to refute his assertion.

"Although I do not know how she came by her information, she repeated it to you in its worst possible light," he continued. "Trust me when I tell you that you are much admired by the gentlemen of London society, and much envied by the women."

Jillian's chin lifted. "I think you mean I'm sneered at and reviled for being the daughter of a merchant."

"That is Sophia's malice at work, Miss Roring. Like me, the gentlemen of my acquaintance hold the Ice Captain in high esteem."

"And my nickname? What do you have to say to that?"

"I've already told you, Ice Princess was a term of the utmost admiration and an homage to Captain Roring. Sophia has twisted the whole of this entire business to damage any regard you might have for me."

"Why on Earth would she do such a thing?"

"Because it was *I* who ended the engagement, Miss Roring, not her."

"What?"

"I caught her in a compromising position with Lord Archibald. I broke our engagement and the scoundrel refused to marry her."

Jillian's fingers tightened in Logan's as she fought to keep her footing. His strong arms steadied her.

"I never meant to reveal this to anyone, but Sophia has forced my hand," he said.

"H-How can I be certain *you* are not twisting the truth?"

His dazzling smile grabbed her heart and held it fast, even as the waltz came to a close.

"Reflect on your observations of the people involved and draw your own conclusions, Miss Roring."

The music ended. Logan escorted her back to Aunt Letty and bowed.

"Thank you for the dance," he said. "I hope to repeat the pleasure very soon."

As he walked away, Aunt Letty rose from her seat. "I could use some rum punch."

JILLIAN SAMPLED the tangy cold liquid in the cup, shuddered, and handed it back to her aunt. "It's too strong."

Aunt Letty sipped the punch. "It's perfect."

"I noticed Mr. Logan speaking with you earlier."

"Yes, indeed. He told me a very scandalous tale as a matter of fact. From the expression on your face while you were dancing with him just now, I assume he related the same story to you."

"He did, and I'm bewildered. Do you suppose his story can be believed?"

"Mr. Logan would be an incorrigible cad to blacken the names of Lord Archibald and Miss Watkins in such an infamous fashion. Since he has always acted in a respectable manner before, I must therefore conclude he is telling the truth."

"But Archie does not seem wicked."

"How can you make a sound conclusion on such a short acquaintance?"

"You are right, I cannot. There is no love lost between Mr. Logan and Archie, however. Only the thinnest veneer of civility prevented them from fisticuffs."

Aunt Letty's face lit up.

"To have two such men openly fight over you would set tongues wagging for years. It would be a quite a triumph."

"Oh, Aunt, don't joke about such things. How am I to decide who is the better man?"

Aunt Letty raised her cup in a toast.

"Dance and be merry, Jillian. It will all become clear in the end."

HONOR AND VIRTUE

*J*n the first half of the ball, Jillian danced twice with Lord Archibald and once with his father, the Duke of Rochester. Stares and whispers seemed to accompany her every movement. During the final lanciers before intermission, a girl deliberately trod on her dress. It was only by the swift intervention of Jillian's partner, Mr. Loach, that the gown escaped damage.

"Have a care, Miss Roring," he said as he led her off the dance floor afterward. "It seems the knives have been sharpened."

"Oh, dear."

"It was the same with your mother, you know."

Jillian's eyebrows lifted. "You knew my mother?"

"Oh, yes, quite well. She was a great beauty, and I was very fond of her. At one party, a certain young lady was so envious, she dropped a cup of tea on your mother's white dress."

"What did my mother do?"

"She sponged the tea off in the ladies' sitting room and was very gracious about it." He chuckled. "But her best revenge was in marrying your father."

Jillian laughed. "Papa will be in London shortly. He shall escort me to Lady Adams's ball."

"And no doubt he will outshine all the other gentlemen in attendance."

A trio of young ladies surrounded Jillian just then, giggling. Although they had all been introduced to her throughout the evening, she didn't know any of them particularly well.

"I see it is time for me to leave you." Mr. Loach bowed to Jillian. "Thank you for the dance." He joined the crowd heading for the banquet hall.

"Miss Roring, we are walking to the garden for some fresh air," said Miss Dooney. "Will you accompany us?"

"Erm…" Jillian glanced toward Aunt Letty, but her chair was empty. "Actually, a little fresh air would be welcome. As long as we stay together, I suppose no harm will arise."

After the warmth of the ballroom, the night air was refreshing. A full complement of stars accented the sky, and a warm spring breeze made the flowers dance.

"Let's go to the gazebo in the center," suggested Miss Taylor. "There's a beautiful view of the house from there."

As they walked, the girls peppered Jillian with questions about her gown and hair, which dance she'd enjoyed most, and whether or not any particular gentleman had caught her eye. Laughing, she answered their questions as best she could, but deflected the question about gentlemen.

"I heard Lord Archibald kissed your hand." Miss Byron sighed. "I would swoon if he kissed mine."

A waterfall of giggles accompanied her remarks. The path to the gazebo was circuitous, winding its way around several tall trees and shrubs. Jillian glanced back toward the house at one point, but a hedge obscured her view.

"I'm glad you're all with me. I should become lost out here in the dark," she said.

"It would be ever so much fun if we played hide and seek," said Miss Dooney.

"We don't have time for that," Jillian said. "The dancing resumes in another ten minutes."

Fortunately, the gazebo was just up ahead. The girls climbed the steps onto the round, wide platform and enjoyed the view of the well-lit mansion. Jillian leaned against the railing, closed her eyes, and breathed in the fragrance of the nearby roses.

"This is such a beautiful home," she said. "And I adore the garden."

Jillian turned around to see why no one had replied, but her companions had disappeared.

SOPHIA and her mother lingered in the ballroom chatting with Lady Adams as the intermission began. A group of giggling girls suddenly herded an unsuspecting Jillian past. They left the ballroom through the doorway leading to the garden. Although neither Lady Adams nor Mrs. Watkins saw anything amiss, Sophia could guess what was about to transpire. She brushed off a pang of guilt. With a concerted effort, Sophia refocused her attention on Lady Adams, who was speaking about her own upcoming event.

"The servants ran out of bees' wax halfway through polishing the ballroom floor, can you believe it?"

"Oh, no!" Mrs. Watkins exclaimed. "Were you able to buy more?"

"Do you realize how difficult it is to procure bees' wax during the Season? I had to send a servant out to our country house to retrieve a quantity from storage."

Without warning, Sophia stomped her foot. "Oh, bother."

"Indeed, it was," Lady Adams said. "But it will all be worth it in the end."

"Excuse me, Lady Adams. Excuse me, Mum." Sophia curtsied. "There is someone I must speak with."

"But, Sophia..."

She hastened from the room, oblivious to her mother's protests. The hallway was filled with people, and still more filled the banquet hall. Sophia craned her neck, looking for Logan. He was nowhere to be seen, but she did spy Hawkins as he was seating Miss Kelsey at a table. Composing a pleasant, calm expression, she approached.

"Mr. Hawkins, I wonder if you might know where Mr. Logan has gone?"

"I believe he went to the cloakroom, Miss Watkins. He may have already left."

Sophia whirled around almost before Hawkins had finished speaking and moved as quickly as decorum would allow. Logan emerged from the cloakroom as she arrived; his cloak draped over one arm and his hat in hand.

"Logan, I need your help."

"Miss Watkins, right now you are the last person to whom I'd wish to render assistance."

"Upon my honor, this is a matter of urgency."

One of his eyebrows lifted. "Forgive me for saying so, but your honor isn't worth two shillings."

"Oh, all right, I suppose I deserve that. But this isn't about me, it's about Miss Roring."

As he peered at Sophia, Logan's eyes narrowed with suspicion.

~

THE GAZEBO WAS empty and Jillian was alone.

"Where has everyone gone? Miss Hanna? Miss Grassley? This is really no time for hide and seek."

Silence was her response, although she thought she could

hear giggles in the distance. Jillian groaned. She'd just had a practical joke played on her. *Why didn't I heed Mr. Loach's warning?*

Before she could leave, Lord Archibald bounded into the gazebo. "What on Earth are you doing here all alone, Miss Roring?"

"I've been abandoned by my friends, I'm afraid. Will you take me back to the house?"

"Certainly. It's a good thing I decided to go for a walk." He closed the distance between them. "May I tell you how enchanting you look in the moonlight?" He reached out to caress her face but she stepped away.

"I'm sorry, Archie, but this isn't at all proper."

He pouted. "Don't you like me, Miss Roring? Even a little?"

"That is beside the point."

His straight white teeth gleamed in the light reflected from the house. "So you *do* like me."

"Lord Archibald, I beg you to escort me to my aunt before she becomes concerned about my absence."

Archie advanced. Jillian backed up until a wooden column cut off her escape.

"How providential," he murmured.

He leaned in for a kiss, but she pushed him away with surprising strength. A few threads on her gown popped with the effort.

"That is enough!" she exclaimed. "I'll find my own way back."

Jillian tried to flee, but Archie caught her by the arm. She was about to slap him when someone stepped out of the darkness, grabbed Archie by the scruff of his neck, and hauled him off. Jillian gasped when she realized it was Logan.

"Archie, you're a libertine and I've been aching to thrash you since our university days," he said.

"How deliciously common of you," Lord Archibald replied. "Let's have at it."

Logan shrugged off his cutaway jacket, tossed it aside, and then clouted Archie on the jaw with his bare knuckles. Archie staggered backward, shook his head to clear it, and then lunged at Logan. As the two men fought, Sophia darted around the combatants and dragged a stunned Jillian from the gazebo to safety.

"Should...shouldn't we get some help?" Jillian squeaked.

"No," Sophia replied. Her calmness seemed out of place. "Logan was a champion boxer in school and Archie has it coming to him."

To Jillian, the fight lasted forever. In reality, it went on only for a half-minute or so. Logan took a several blows to the face and stomach, but he inflicted more punishment than he received. Archie finally sank down to his knees.

"Maybe this will teach you not to impose yourself on a lady," Logan said.

A roundhouse punch to the face knocked Archie unconscious. Logan bent nearly double as he tried to regain his breath. Jillian and Sophia hastened into the gazebo. While Sophia checked on Archie, Jillian put a hand on Logan's shoulder.

"Are you all right?"

Logan straightened. He appeared to have suffered a blackened eye and bleeding knuckles, but a grin lit his face. As he pulled a handkerchief from a pocket and wrapped it around his hand, he was positively cheerful.

"Archie's teeth cut my knuckles, but it was worth it. More importantly, are *you* all right, Miss Roring?"

"Besides feeling exceptionally foolish, I am fine. How did you and Sophia come to be here?" Her eyes slid from Logan to Sophia, and she couldn't suppress a gasp. *He brought her out here for privacy!* "Oh...of course."

"No, Jillian, you have it wrong," Sophia said. "I noticed the girls planning to play a trick on you and I knew Archie was part of it. I pressed Logan for his assistance."

"How could you possibly know Archie was planning to take advantage of me?" Jillian asked, bewildered.

"Because he did the same thing to me last year. Only in my case, I was willing," Sophia said. Her cheeks reddened, and her eyes dropped to the gazebo floor.

As Jillian gazed at Logan, her heart soared.

"It seems you've rescued me yet again," she said. "I am in your debt, and the ledger balance grows daily."

He took her into his arms and cradled her in a tender embrace.

"It is you who have rescued me, Miss Roring. I was bitter and angry before—dare I say melancholy? But you have changed my heart."

Sophia's mouth dropped open.

"Are you more acquainted with one other than you have confessed?"

Jillian and Logan laughed.

"A little," they said together.

"I suppose we've all been keeping secrets." Sophia smiled. "Let me escort you both back to the ball so there is no scandal, and then I shall fetch servants to come to Archie's aid. It's such a shame he had too much to drink and tripped in the dark at his own party."

"A terrible shame," Jillian agreed.

"The sad event has freed up Miss Roring's dance card considerably, though," Logan added. "It's an ill wind that blows no good."

NEEDLE AND THREAD IN HAND, Sophia checked Jillian's dress in the ladies' sitting room.

"Give a little twirl for me."

Jillian turned, slowly.

"Yes, you are fine again. There was just a little rip under one arm." Sophia gave the needle and thread back to the attendant.

"Thank you." Jillian searched Sophia's face. "Why are you helping me?"

"I believe my long-neglected sense of decency finally rose from the dead. I repaid your friendship with malice and I'm heartily ashamed of it. Can you ever forgive me? I've acted abominably."

With a smile, Jillian extended her hand. "It's as you said before. I think we should be good friends."

Sophia and Jillian sailed into the ballroom together, where the rest of the evening lay before them. Vicar Lewis brightened when he saw Sophia. To Jillian's surprise, Sophia greeted him warmly.

"Vicar, do you know what I heard just now? My dear friends Miss Grassley, Miss Hanna, and Miss Byron were near coming to blows. I believe they may be a little in love with you."

"Truly?" The vicar was flustered.

"If you were to dance with each girl, it would be a very Christian thing to do."

"Why, yes. I shall apply myself to the task right away."

The vicar hastened off toward Miss Hanna, who was standing alone next to a candelabra. As the orchestra readied their instruments for a polka, Logan appeared at Jillian's elbow. He had washed up and looked presentable, excepting the faint blue swelling on one cheekbone. As he gazed at Jillian with eyes full of longing, her knees grew weak. He bowed and offered her his arm. "May I have this dance?"

THE ICE CAPTAIN RETURNS

The first few days of the ocean voyage, Betsy stayed in her small, elegantly appointed cabin. Although seasickness accounted for a portion of her confinement, the larger part was the crippling knowledge she did not truly fit in with the first class passengers. She spent her time trying to iron out her Cockney accent.

"I'm happy ter—*to*—make yer—*you're*—acquaintance, sir. Madam, them's—*those*—are beautiful pearls *you're* wearing. It's foin—*fine*—weather we're having lately."

On the fourth day, however, she rallied enough to take breakfast in the common room. She spoke with no one except the waiter but did manage to observe and emulate the manners of the other ladies as best she could. With slightly elevated confidence, she joined the other passengers strolling on the deck of the ship. Her jaw dropped at the sight of the Atlantic, which looked a great deal larger on deck than it had from her porthole. Dizziness swept over her when she realized there was nothing below the ship's hull except miles of water. A passing gentleman caught her as she swayed.

"Are you unwell, miss? Would you like me to get help?"

Betsy gazed into the man's earnest, bespectacled face. He was perhaps a few years older than she was, with a pleasant appearance. She cleared her throat.

"I'm *fine*, sir. Perhaps a bit o'—er, *of* sea sickness."

"Ah. I suffered the same, but I am doing better now." He lifted his hat. "Good day to you, madam."

As he turned to leave, Betsy slipped his purloined wallet into her reticule. She bit her lip, instantly regretting her actions. *Why did I do that? Ladies do not pick pockets!* A nearby deck chair beckoned, and she sank onto it. Wispy white clouds scraped the blue skies overhead, as if forming the slightest of barriers between her and heaven. Were she a sparrow, only the slightest change of course would put her on the other side.

A little boy in a sailor suit, perhaps six years old, skidded to a stop next to her chair. He stared at her hat with gray, serious eyes, and pointed at the tiny decorative roses on the crown. "Are those for real?"

It took Betsy a moment to figure out what he was asking. "Oh, no. The flowers are made from ribbon."

He nodded, once. "You're pretty."

A crooked smile lit her face. "Thank you." She glanced up and down the deck but saw no matrons young enough to be the boy's mother or governess. "Where's your mum?"

"She died."

Her heart melted. "Oh! I'm awfully sorry. Where's your father, then?"

The boy's mouth split open in a mischievous grin. One of his front teeth was missing. "It's time for lessons, so I gave Papa the slip."

"He will be looking for you."

"We're going to America, Papa and I. He's says we're starting a whole new life."

"Aye…I mean *yes*. That's me as well."

"I'm a bit scared, but it's exciting too. I want to see an Indian." He studied her a moment, and then made her a little bow. "My name is Kevin Moorecock. I'm pleased to make your acquaintance."

Betsy nodded and smiled. "Miss Abernathy."

Just then, the boy's father hurried over; it was the same gentleman who'd spoken to her a few minutes earlier.

"There you are, Kevin! I was worried you'd fallen overboard."

"Miss Abernathy, allow me to introduce you to Papa," the boy said. "Papa, this is my new friend. We're all going to America together."

"Mr. Moorecock, at your service," he said, bowing. "Thank you for looking after my son."

The man took Kevin by the hand and they headed off.

"Excuse me, Mr. Moorecock," Betsy called out. When he turned, she held out his wallet. "I believe you must have dropped this."

"Ah, thank you. I didn't realize it was gone. I'm quite grateful to you, Miss Abernathy."

He paused and a scarlet flush spread up from his collar. "W-Would you care to have dinner with K-Kevin and me tonight?"

She gulped back a sudden surge of emotion. "Mr. Moore-cock, I would be delighted."

No champagne was required to lift Jillian's mood as she gazed at her reflection in the looking glass. The diamond necklace and matching earbobs she wore set off her ice blue gown beautifully. Her curled locks had been loosely arranged on top of her head. She turned to smile at her maid.

"You've outdone yourself, Alice. My hair is perfect. Do you know if my father and aunt are ready?"

"I believe they are waiting in the drawing room, miss."

"Could you bring my short Victorine down with you? I don't think I need a wrap, but I suppose I'd better take one anyway."

"Yes, miss."

Jillian gathered up her elbow-length gloves and floated down the stairs on a cloud of ebullience. In the drawing room, Aunt Letty was perched on a sofa, looking splendid in a black and white satin ball gown. Lars Roring stood next to the fireplace, wearing a black cutaway and white vest tailored to his athletic physique. The blond hair brushed back from his handsome face was only slightly touched by gray. His bright blue eyes, now etched by faint lines, twinkled when his daughter entered the room.

"With you and Letty on my arm, I shall be the most envied man at the ball tonight," he said in lightly accented English.

Jillian hugged him. "I'm so pleased you're escorting us. I was a bit worried you wouldn't be here on time."

Aunt Letty gave Lars a sidelong glance. "I know a few ladies who will be interested to know you are retiring from the sea."

The captain's deep masculine laugh filled the drawing room. "I've only been in London a day and already with the match-making, Letty?"

"Why not?" Jillian asked. "You are still young, Papa. Besides, you'll have plenty of opportunities to circulate in London society while you supervise construction of the new ice factory."

Smiling, Roring picked up his top hat and cape and gestured toward the door.

"After you, ladies."

SOPHIA and her mother strolled around Lady Adams's ballroom, both to admire the floral decorations and to display Sophia's violet gown to the gentlemen assembled there. The skirt had three flounces and emphasized her tiny waist. Her hair had been dressed with several small satin flowers the same color as her dress.

"You've never looked better, Sophia," her mother murmured. "Just be sure to hold your shoulders back."

"Yes, Mama."

Suddenly there was an excited murmur at the ballroom entrance.

"I wonder who has arrived?" Sophia asked.

"Perhaps it is the Duke and Duchess of Rochester," Mrs. Watkins replied.

"I hope not," Sophia said. "They have the unfortunate tendency to bring Archie with them." She craned her neck. "Could it be Prince Albert Edward himself?"

Mrs. Watkins inhaled sharply. Sophia followed her gaze. Standing next to Jillian and Mrs. Marsh was the most gorgeous older man she'd ever seen. His startlingly blond hair reflected the light and his high, sculpted cheekbones begged to be touched.

"Who is *that*, Mum?" she exclaimed.

Mrs. Watkins sighed and fanned herself with a beautiful lace fan. "The one who got away, dear."

JILLIAN GIGGLED INWARDLY at all the melting glances her father was receiving. Even Lady Adams had simpered like a schoolgirl when he'd greeted her in the receiving line. Mr. Loach came over to shake his hand and to introduce the Ice Captain to his wife. Although it had been nearly twenty years since Lars Roring had been seen in society, his friends had not forgotten him. As the ladies and gentlemen of London society surrounded her father, Jillian discretely stepped back.

"Good evening, Miss Roring."

She looked up into a pair of Gypsy eyes, and her pulse began to race.

"Good evening, Mr. Logan."

"Will you walk with me onto the balcony? It has a lovely view of the garden."

"I should dearly love to see the view, despite the fact that it's completely dark outside."

Logan escorted her through the double doors leading to a large balcony, where a floral garland scented the air with heady fragrance. At the railing, Logan stood behind Jillian and slipped his arms around her waist. She closed her eyes and leaned back against him.

"Miss Roring, I can't seem to stop bothering you, can I?" he murmured.

As he trailed little kisses down her neck, exquisite sensations surged through her body. She reached up to caress his face with her hand.

"You're not a bother, Mr. Logan. In fact, I beg you to continue."

"To do so would compromise my honor, unless…well, unless we were married. I love you, Jillian. Say you'll have me."

At that, she turned around. Logan gazed at her with a soft and vulnerable expression that turned her insides to molten gold.

"I believe I will have you, Mackenzie."

As they kissed, she surrendered her heart.

The End

EPILOGUE

TWO YEARS LATER

*J*illian and Logan stood at the entrance of the nursery, watching as Mrs. Lyman rocked the cradle holding their newborn daughter. The adoring expression on the older woman's face lent it an unaccustomed sweetness.

"I still can't believe we have our own little ice princess," Logan whispered.

The housekeeper gave him a scorching glare and made a shushing noise. Giggling, Jillian pulled her husband away from the door. They walked down the stairs together, hand in hand.

"Hawkins and Katie are coming for dinner tonight. It's just a guess, but I suspect they have some news to share," she said.

"Such as?"

"Katie's been growing plump."

He chortled. "A baby?"

"We'll know soon enough. Try to act surprised."

Not fifteen minutes later, Jillian's uncle came to call with a package under his arm. Jillian's eyes lit up. "A present for me?"

"I have no idea," Sir William replied. "It arrived yesterday from America, but there is no return address."

"From America? How very strange," she said.

"Why don't you open it, Jillian? Sir William, would you fancy a game of billiards?" Logan asked.

"Certainly, my boy, but don't you ever get tired of losing?"

The two men headed off into the game room while Jillian brought her package into the library. Underneath the paper wrapping was a cardboard box containing her gold earbobs and jeweled hatpin. There was also a note, written in large, rounded script. Bewildered, she brought the note over to the window to read.

Dear Miss Roring,

This here is Betsy and I am writing from my new home in America. I started my life over here. I'm married now, to a decent man who does not drink or hit me. He has a wonderful little boy I love like he was my own. I also learned how to read and write and act like a lady.

I have to unburden myself by begging your forgiveness. What George, Sam and I did was wrong, but I can't take it back. I am returning your earbobs and hatpin, hoping you will understand how sorry I am.

Yours ever,

Betsy

The gold earbobs sparkled in the light streaming through the window. Jillian examined the hatpin, remembering how it had made such an effective weapon when she had needed it. Now she would be able to pass it on to her own daughter, with an amusing story.

She left the wrappings where they were and hastened into the game room with Betsy's letter and recovered treasures.

"Look! Betsy returned these things to me, after all this time."

She interrupted Logan as he was trying to sink a shot. The cue hit the ball off center and the shot went awry. Jillian winced. "Sorry. That was my fault."

"Don't give him an excuse," Sir William said.

"I'm glad you got your things back," Logan said. "I know that hatpin had sentimental value."

"Yes, but it also means Betsy has decided to be a good person. I'm glad to know people can change."

As Sir William bent over the pool table, Logan took Jillian in his arms.

"I'm glad to know some things will never change."

They exchanged a long, romantic kiss.

ABOUT THE AUTHOR

 Suzanne G. Rogers is a California native, but she changed coastlines and now lives in romantic Savannah, Georgia, on an island populated by deer, exotic birds, turtles, otters, and gators.

SNEAK PEEK AT JESSAMINE'S FOLLY

"Love is the wisdom of the fool and the folly of the wise."
– Samuel Johnson

After her estate is entailed away, Jessamine Foster has no choice but to live with relatives who detest her. When her aunt gives her an ultimatum to leave, Jessamine accepts a position as companion to Lord Kirkendale's sister—even though she's been warned her predecessors can't seem to resist the earl's exceptional good looks. Can Jessamine manage to hold onto her job without losing her heart?

To honor a promise made to his dying father, Lord Kirkendale agrees to an arranged marriage to a woman he cannot love. Although he is resigned to a life without sentiment, the arrival of his sister's new companion awakens a slumbering passion. Can he find a way to secure his own happiness without sacrificing his family's honor, or will his broken promise result in the ruination of the person he loves most?

Keep reading for an excerpt...

MISFORTUNE

NOVEMBER, 1902. DERBYSHIRE, ENGLAND.

*S*wathed in a black veil, Lillian sat alone in the back of the church. As young Jessamine Foster made her way up the aisle after the funeral service, pale and forlorn, Lillian's heart bled. When Jessamine passed by, her gaze lingered on Lillian's face. Startled, Lillian averted her eyes and bowed her head—as if in prayer. *I've never regretted my decisions before—until now. If circumstances were different, I would take her into my home and give her the world.* Even at age fifteen, the girl showed signs of great beauty and good breeding. After her debut in three years, she could make a splendid marriage. *Any connection with me would spoil her chances.*

Moments later, Jessamine's Uncle Thackery followed Jessamine from the church. Next came Thackery's wife Rachel and daughter Charlotte—who appeared to be about Jessamine's age. Certainly, the Fosters would look after Jessamine and make sure her launch into Society was managed well. *I can be a silent benefactor, at least. The poor girl will want for nothing and be comforted in the knowledge she has someone who cares—even if we never meet.*

~

MOURNERS POURED into Arbor Manor after the double funeral for Jesse and Minerva Foster, clad in black and wreathed in sorrow. Numb, Jessamine barely heard their expressions of condolences, although she forced herself to nod and express gratitude like her parents would have wished. Fortunately, the staff did an impeccable job serving refreshments, so she didn't have to worry about playing hostess. Jessamine's aunt seemed to warm to the task, however, although her high-handed manner with the servants set Jessamine's teeth on edge. Cousin Charlotte apparently had gone straight to her room after the carriage returned from the cemetery, since she was nowhere to be seen. Occasionally mourners would glance at Jessamine, shake their heads and whisper things like, "Orphaned at such a tender age, poor girl."

Mr. Abernathy, the family attorney, murmured she was to join him and her uncle for a few moments. Like a puppet on a string, she followed him into the library, where he shut the door. Mr. Thackery Foster was already there, standing with his back toward the fireplace. *How like Papa he is in little ways, and yet not like him in the essentials.* Jessamine sank onto a sofa and tried to listen as Mr. Abernathy explained her financial situation, but his words seemed to be coming at her from a great distance. After his meaning finally sank into her brain, her grief turned to shock. "My father's entire estate is entailed away from me? Surely he made some provision for my future."

"I'm afraid not," Mr. Abernathy said.

"As his attorney, did you not advise him he wouldn't live forever?"

"Repeatedly, Miss Foster. Several months ago I suggested setting aside a sizable dowry on your behalf, but he kept missing our appointments to sign the papers." He shook his head. "This is a terrible tragedy in so many ways."

Panic set in. "Where am I to go?"

"Rest assured, you're welcome at Arbor Manor as long as you like," Mr. Foster said.

"That's very gracious of you, sir," Mr. Abernathy said. "Don't you agree, Miss Foster?"

Although Jessamine opened her mouth to speak, only a strangled sort of moan emerged.

"You and your cousin Charlotte are very close in age," Mr. Abernathy said. "I daresay you'll be like sisters."

The very notion curdled Jessamine's blood. *I cannot bear Charlotte's company for ten minutes! How are we to live under the same roof?* Blinking back tears, she returned to the drawing room. As she glanced around the elegantly appointed space, taking in its magnificent woodwork, crystal chandeliers, and oriental rugs, her gaze settled on the huge oil painting of her family hanging over the fireplace. *No doubt that will be the first thing to go.*

WITH CRITICAL DETACHMENT, Mrs. Foster watched as two footmen carried Jessamine's family portrait from the drawing room and toward the staircase. "Don't gouge the walls with that horrible thing."

Upon hearing her aunt's voice, Jessamine emerged from the library. Her heart sank as she watched the footmen struggle to lift the unwieldy painting up the staircase. The Fosters had moved into Arbor Manor only two days prior, and already Mrs. Foster was making changes.

"Oh, there you are, Jessamine," Mrs. Foster said. "The maids are moving your parents' clothes and personal effects into the attic. Whatever you don't want, we'll box up for charity. The poor are grateful for any old rag."

"Yes, Aunt."

"Oh, and Charlotte would like a room with a balcony. Since yours is the only one that suits her, you must choose another on the third floor."

A prickle of heat traveled down Jessamine's spine. "There are fifteen bedrooms in this house, and several of them have lovely views of the garden. Surely Charlotte will be content with one of them."

The tight smile on Mrs. Foster's lips never reached her eyes. "The sooner you realize this is *our* house now, the better. Your uncle has been generous enough to give you a place to live and food from our table. You should be grateful."

"I *am* grateful—to my uncle," Jessamine retorted. *Your good fortune is at my expense, and you're not even gracious about it!*

Mrs. Foster's nostrils flared. "I'll thank you to keep a civil tongue in your head."

Jessamine's cousin appeared on the landing just then, clad in an off-the-shoulder silk gown with a floating skirt of white tulle. "Mama, isn't this the most beautiful dress you've ever seen?"

Delighted, Mrs. Foster clasped her hands together. "Oh, don't you look gorgeous!"

Jessamine gasped. "Where did you find that dress? You can't have it!"

As she descended the stairs past the footmen, Charlotte's smirk lent an ugly cast to her pretty face. "Why not? It was hanging in one of the spare rooms, and everything in this house belongs to Papa now."

"Not exactly. That was the dress my mother wore when she was presented to the queen," Jessamine said. "I was to wear it for my debut."

"You're not to have a debut anymore, so I should have it." Charlotte's smug tone was insufferable. "Don't be so selfish, cousin."

Jessamine spoke through gritted teeth. "Take it off right now."

"Mama?" Charlotte pleaded. "Make her see reason."

"Charlotte is right, Jessamine," Mrs. Foster said. "You won't have a Season, so you don't need the gown. Think about someone else for once in your miserable life and let her have it."

As her aunt spoke, something inside Jessamine snapped. She advanced on Charlotte with her fists clenched at her side. "Take it off or I'll *make* you take it off."

"Jessamine Anastasia Foster, how dare you speak to Charlotte like that!" Mrs. Foster exclaimed.

Mrs. Foster fluttered in the background as the two girls glared at one another for several long, hostile moments.

"Fine," Charlotte said finally. "I won't wear it then."

She reached across the bodice, grasped one of the puffy gossamer sleeves, and gave it a vicious tug. The fabric and the trim ripped, sending beads raining to the floor. The next thing Jessamine knew, her hand flew out and slapped Charlotte across the face. The footmen had reached the landing at that point, but nearly dropped the painting as they craned their necks to watch the conflict. Her cousin and aunt shrieked, but Jessamine brushed past them and mounted the stairs.

"You're a wicked girl, Jessamine Foster!" Mrs. Foster exclaimed.

ALSO BY SUZANNE G. ROGERS

HISTORICAL ROMANCE

An American in Paris of the West

Rumer Has It

One Little Kiss

Courtship on Eaton Square

The Prettier Sister

The Glass Heart

*Audiobook Available

ALSO BY SUZANNE G. ROGERS

FANTASY

The Yden Series

The Last Great Wizard of Yden (Book One)

Dragon Clan of Yden (Book Two)

Secrets of Yden (Book Three)

Kira (Prequel to the Yden Trilogy)

Standalone Titles

Dani & the Immortals

*The Dragon Rider's Daughter**

Clash of Wills

Tournament of Chance: Dragon Rebel

Magical Misperception

*Whimsical Tendencies**

Something Wicked in L.A.

Royal Promenade

*Audiobook Available

www.ingramcontent.com/pod-product-compliance
Lightning Source LLC
Chambersburg PA
CBHW072229190626
46809CB00017B/1544